PAYTIME FOR A GOOD MAN

Todd Coulter was a good, family man, who abided by the laws of God and lived by honest toil. But eventually he lost his family, his home and everything he'd worked for. Then someone from his past turned up showing him a surefire way of making money. Hollis Clarke's methods were dishonest and illegal, but Todd no longer cared. However, they both knew that the day of reckoning always came . . . and when it did — it would be paytime.

JOSEPH JOHN McGRAW

PAYTIME FOR A GOOD MAN

Complete and Unabridged

LINFORD
Leicester

First published in Great Britain in 2011 by
Robert Hale Limited
London

First Linford Edition
published 2013
by arrangement with
Robert Hale Limited
London

British Library CIP Data

McGraw, Joseph John.
    Paytime for a good man.- -
(Linford western library)
1. Western stories.
2. Large type books.
I. Title II. Series
823.9'2–dc23

ISBN 978–1–4448–1420–0

Published by
F. A. Thorpe (Publishing)
Anstey, Leicestershire

Set by Words & Graphics Ltd.
Anstey, Leicestershire
Printed and bound in Great Britain by
T. J. International Ltd., Padstow, Cornwall

This book is printed on acid-free paper

1

Norther

Todd Coulter knew he was pushing the horse beyond the limits of endurance. He hated doing it. He was not a cruel man. But more was at stake than the life of a horse.

He spurred hard up Shelton Heights. Below and ahead of him, the trail unfolded like a powdery white ribbon over the sandy plain, which stretched away yellow on either side. It curled into the distance, skirting rocky outcrops and disappearing at moments in folds in the land. Blocking his view, Scott's Mesa sprang vertically two hundred feet into the air. But beyond it was Clanton. And hope. Another three miles.

He hesitated. If he had any heart or

even sense, he'd give the horse a breather, a couple of minutes to get its wind back before forcing it on. But if he did that, it might jib, dig in, lie down, maybe even roll on him to pay him back. And where would that leave Sarah? He reached for his whip and laid it on hard. The horse flinched then leaped forward again.

The descent from the top of Shelton Heights made the going easier and Todd stopped pushing so hard. When they reached the flat he resisted the temptation to put whip and spur to the animal. No sense in pressing for speed and have the flagging nag die under him, leaving him to slog the rest of the way on foot to where there were people and help. And Sarah needed help. Fast.

He was about level with the mesa when the horse gave a cough, staggered, raced on for another twenty paces before collapsing in the middle of the trail like all its strings had been cut at a stroke. Todd was thrown over its head. He landed on his back and lay there for a moment, winded and dazed. Then he stood up, shook the shooting stars out of his brain and the dust out of his face, his eyes, his clothes. One look and he knew the horse was dead; there was blood trickling out of its ears and nostrils. Its heart had burst. Todd gave it a brief military salute. It had done its job and you had to respect that. Then he turned and started running.

Rounding the mesa, he got his first sight of Clanton, a huddle of mostly single storey clapboard buildings which had grown up like weeds around the newly arrived railway. The town shimmered in the heat. He ran on. Sweat trickled into his eyes and made them sting. He'd run the best part of a mile when he saw a man driving out in a dog cart. Coulter shouted to him. It was Hank Beynon, who ran the livery stable in town. Hank stopped.

'What's up, Todd?'

Without answering, Coulter climbed up beside him then told him his tale in an urgent voice. Hank grunted, turned the cart and urged the draw horse on with reins and whip and did not stop until he was outside Doc Halpern's house.

Doc Halpern was sixty and had a good reputation in Keenan County. Luckily he wasn't out on a call. While he listened as Todd told his tale, he sent Hank off to harness his buggy.

'She's been complaining of a pain in her side on and off for a month or so. It would come and go. We thought it was nothing, that it would go away just like the other times. But this time it didn't go away. It got worse . . . '

'Show me exactly where she said the pain is.'

Todd pointed to a spot low down on his right side, just below his belt.

'Is it tender to the touch?'

'She can't bear any sort of pressure on it.'

'Any sweating?'

'She's drenched in it.'

'Any fever?'

'She's burning up. Says the pain's

agony, nothing I give her or do for her makes it any better. Come on, Doc, you got to do something.'

'I sure do, son. From the way you describe her condition, I'd say your gal has got acute appendicitis. We got to go. Keep praying we're not too late.'

He shouted to Mrs McGuire, his housekeeper, not to wait supper for him, grabbed his hat and put his medical bag in his buggy, which Hank had brought round to the front of the house. While he set off at a lick out of town along the powdery white trail that snaked between the crouching rocks, Hank picked out a horse from the stables. Hank said they could settle up later. With a quick word of thanks, Todd swung up into the saddle.

He soon caught up with Doc Halpern. The buggy was too slow and he was too impatient to be home, too anxious to know Sarah was all right, to tell her the doc was on his way. With a word and a wave, he rode on, up

Shelton Heights and across the plateau where the foothills of the saw-toothed Sierra started to climb into the sky. His spread was in a hollow five miles up ahead, by a stream that flowed down from a valley in back of it.

He'd bought the land just after the War. When the shooting finally stopped and he became a free man again, he'd wandered around the country, punching cows here, working as barkeep there, with no particular aim in view save to keep body and soul together. A ticket on the new railway that was spreading west had eventually brought him to Clanton where he met and fell in love with Sarah. He also fell in love with her uncle's rundown place which snuggled in a hollow in the plateau out beyond Scott's Mesa. The uncle, who was tired of it, had gone back to town and the newly weds moved in. Todd rebuilt the house from the ground up, and he intended it to last. He'd burned limestone like his pa had shown him back home in Colorado, slaked the brittle stone in a pit and mixed the fine lime with sand and water to make mortar. He built the walls of rock but he went to the extra trouble of dressing stone for the chimney. He'd hauled pine logs from higher up in the hills, split them and smoothed them into planks with a broad adze. He used the puncheons for the floor, internal walls and the clapboard roof. He fenced off and ploughed his fields and made a living with the produce of his own toil. At thirty-five, Todd Coulter was proud that he had made something out of nothing.

He and Sarah had been happy from the start. They suited each other and the place suited them. By the time little Phil came along, the years he had spent in uniform and the horrors he'd seen in the war had more or less faded from his mind. It seemed to him that they lived charmed lives. The farm prospered and Phil grew strong and confident. Then one day, when he was three, he trod on a rattler and was dead before they knew what was happening. They were starting to make their peace with their loss when Sarah began complaining of the pains in her side . . .

The trail dipped down into the hollow where he'd made his new home and his new life. There was smoke at his chimney and someone sitting by the door. But it wasn't Sarah. It was Mick Murphy. He'd left her with Mick and his wife Annie, their nearest neighbours and good friends. Mick saw him, didn't wave, but stood up and went inside the house. When he came out again, Annie came with him. Todd didn't have to blink and look again: he knew.

He walked his sweating horse the rest of the way. There was no need for hurry now.

Annie came to meet him.

'She's gone, Todd. The pain just got too much and in the end she passed out. Couldn't wake her. We used wet cloths to keep the fever down. But she breathed slower and slower until she wasn't breathing at all. But she's not suffering now.'

Without speaking, Todd went into the house. Sarah was lying perfectly still on their bed. She looked like she always did when she was sleeping.

He stayed a while, then went outside.

When Doc Halpern arrived, it was Annie Murphy who broke the news. The doc took a look at Sarah, just in case.

'Septicaemia,' he said. 'It's a big word to die of. But it means her blood was poisoned. It was her appendix sure enough. When it bursts like that, the badness just backs up and they don't last long.'

'Todd's taking it bad,' said Mick. 'He ain't said much, but anyone can see how hard he's been hit.'

Before the doc started off back to town, Annie made him some coffee. Mick called to Todd to ask if he wanted some but got no answer.

Three days later, in Clanton church-yard, Reverend Martin said the words over the grave into which Sarah Coulter, twenty-eight, loving wife, had been lowered in her coffin.

Todd couldn't believe it. Sarah had been taken from him while the world was still full of cruel, selfish, black-hearted people.

★   ★   ★

In the days and weeks that followed, Mick and Annie would drop by the Coulter place. At first, their visits passed in silence. Annie would bring a pan with a stew or a cloth-covered plate of biscuits she had baked. Sometimes, she put what she'd brought on the table next to the pie or meatloaf she'd left on her last visit, which Todd had left untouched. She was a good-hearted woman and was never offended. She even tidied the place up while Mick saw to the animals. Sooner or later, their friend would pull through, start up again, make a new life for himself.

Later, he became aware of their kindness and said how he appreciated it.

'What you going to do now, Todd?' asked Annie. 'You intending to stay on here?'

'You could sell up and move on, make a fresh start somewhere else,' said Mick.

'I got too much past invested in this place to be thinking of walking out on what Sarah and I made here. Maybe I'll get round to it later.'

'Life hasn't been kind to you,' said Annie.

She was right. First, there'd been the war. He'd fought on the side of right, but there'd been too much blood. He'd seen things that made him sick to the stomach and he'd done things he wasn't proud of and tried not to remember. Then there was Phil, the innocent victim of a cruel world. And now Sarah . . . Three things. Mick said bad luck comes in threes, then left a person alone for a spell. Maybe his luck would turn now. Todd wasn't sure he much cared if it did or not.

Slowly he got back into a routine and Mick and Annie didn't feel they had to come by so often. Maybe he needed to be by himself to come to terms with his new life. And so the year moved from spring to summer and the new season's heat took hold of those southern skies.

Of an evening, he would climb up to the top of the hill where he and Sarah used to sit sometimes and watch their very own sunset together. On one stifling evening, he sat with his knees drawn up to his chin watching the view. Below was his house. Around it, the yellowing corn was high and to his left his half-dozen steers were grazing peacefully.

Maybe Mick had been right, he mused. Maybe it was time to move on. He had no roots in Clanton, Keenan County, no folks except Sarah's old uncle who wasn't blood kin anyway. What he'd built with his bare hands had no meaning now he was on his own again. He felt a sudden stab of the old wanderlust that had taken him as a boy away from Colorado to see the world. He'd thought he'd done with wandering. He'd wandered enough to know that however far you travel you never get far from yourself. So why was he feeling uneasy?

Then he knew why. Everything around him had gone quiet. There was an edgy, threatening feel to things. His steers had stopped grazing and had gone into a huddle; the sky had darkened and though there were a couple of hours still to go before sundown, it felt like night. A great pewter cloud hung overhead like a lid on a pan; the air was still and the heat was becoming unbearable. As Todd wiped the sweat out of his eyes one more time, his face was suddenly caressed by a puff of cool breeze, then scraped by a bitter chill, then slapped by a freezing hand. The first faint movement of cold air was followed by a series of strong gusts which turned into a wider respiration as though the whole earth was struggling to breathe through the rapid drop in temperature. What Todd felt against his skin he could also see the effects of in the glade below him. His animals moved into the shelter of the trees that marked the boundary of his land and the corn in his fields swayed, bent low and then lay flat, as though it had been swept by a giant hand wielding an invisible brush. And then everything around him started moving.

Todd recognized the signs, though he'd never seen a norther before. They start after a hot day and the temperature could drop fifty or sixty degrees in no time at all. Teamsters, herdsmen and travellers caught in the open often perished, and animals suffered intensely. Cattle instinctively made for the shelter of trees; but on the open prairie, they died in their thousands from a soaking by a freezing rain which was sometimes added to the devil's brew.

The rushing air snatched at his shirt,

whipped the cloth of his pants, tore at his hair. He had to find shelter. To his left, thirty yards down the slope, was the cave where he and Sarah had sometimes slept in the early days, because it was fun or cool there or because they wanted to stay dry on rainy nights before he'd fixed the clapboard on the roof-timbers of the house. He'd just got inside when the hillside was swept by a blast that would have taken the sails off a ship and snapped its masts. It was as cold as if it had been blowing across a sea of ice. Then the norther opened the sluices.

Without warning there was water everywhere. It ran in wild torrents down the hill, gouged deep channels in the earth and cascaded over the entrance to the cave like a waterfall. Todd could see nothing except the brilliant flashes of lightning which pierced the crashing gloom. He had to cover his ears to protect them against the booming thunder and the constant roar of rushing water. This was not weather, he thought, it was the judgement of the Lord. But what sins was the Almighty bent on punishing out here, on the edge of Keenan County?

The flood eased but not the intensity of the storm. The gloom lifted and through the roar he heard what seemed like a great rattle of old bones. Then a hailstone the size of a small rock bounced into the cave and landed at his feet. Todd suddenly felt very angry. Mick's rule of three applied to others but not to him — he took it personal. He picked up the hailstone in a rage and hurled it back into the teeth of the storm. But others followed it in. He picked those up too and flung them in the face of wind and rain. He made it his mission to send those hailstones back where they came from. 'The judgement of the Lord is in the earth!' The phrase went round his head and every hailstone he threw was his way of fighting against the sentence that had been passed on him.

The violence of the hailstorm stopped as suddenly as it had begun, the pewter cloud lightened and lifted but the flashing and booming continued unabated. The veil of driving, slanting rain eased for a moment and he saw three of his cows killed as lightning lopped a huge limb from the tree under which they had sought shelter. Through another gap in the rain, he saw that the stream which ran past the house had become a raging torrent. He stepped outside the cave but was forced back by the strength of the wind. Breathing after his exertions, Todd sat on his haunches to wait until the norther moved on.

It blew itself out an hour later.

The wind died to nothing, the temperature rose and the sky glowed in the crimson sunset which ended most days of most weeks of every summer Todd had known for as long as he'd lived in his glen. But the place didn't smell or feel or look the same because it wasn't. His animals were all dead, his fences not just destroyed but gone, his trees not just uprooted but reduced to splinters, fields no longer green but torn up and brown, as if they'd been newly ploughed by a mad farmhand. The destruction was total. Not much was left of the house; the roof had gone and the walls had been blown down. Only the chimney was left standing.

He climbed down the hill where the cascading water had dug deep trenches and rolled boulders into the valley bottom. He crossed the stream, no longer a raging torrent, but once more the busy brook it had been only hours before.

He was sitting on what was left of the east wall of his house when Mick and Annie arrived.

'My God!' breathed Mick, awed by the devastation, 'you got the brunt of it! I never saw anything like this.'

'We got off lightly,' said Annie, 'and we're only a couple of miles away.'

'It's all gone,' said Todd. 'Call me Jonah.'

'No good talking like that, Todd,' said Mick. 'Tomorrow is another day and the next step is always forward. Stay and put things right. Or sell up and move on. You're your own man. You decide.'

'To be sure,' said Annie. 'But first, you stay with us tonight. You'll see things clearer in the morning.'

Todd straightened and stood up.

'Thanks for the invite, Annie, but I think I'll ride into town. I'm not a drinking man but tonight I'm going to get very, very drunk. I'll sleep where I fall.'

The most help he would accept was the loan of a horse, for all his animals were dead or had run away and were probably still running. He rode un-hurriedly, unseeingly into Clanton. Something in his head kept telling him that the judgement of the Lord was in the Earth. He was counting on whiskey to make the words go away.

The storm had missed Clanton altogether. It was dark and the streets were almost empty, but the saloon was busy. He strode up to the bar and ordered rye whiskey.

The barkeep slopped a measure into a glass and returned the cork to the neck of the bottle and the bottle to its shelf all in one smooth action. Todd reached for his drink and sank it in one. He slammed the glass down hard on the counter and said:

'Same again.'

The barkeep jumped to it. He was about to complete his trick and put the bottle back where it belonged when a voice at Todd's elbow said:

'Pour one for me — and leave the bottle.'

Todd turned and found himself looking into a face he hadn't seen in half a dozen years. The face grinned. Todd grinned back.

'Hollis Clarke! What in tarnation are you doing here?'

2

A Face From the Past

'I came looking for you, soldier.'

'Good to see you, soldier.'

'I brought some ammo.'

Todd laughed again, shook Hollis by the hand, took the bottle off the barkeep and led the way to a table at the back of the saloon, where they could be private.

Now it's a fact of life that there are people you think you get close to. But then they drift out of your life and, if they ever drift back into it again, are strangers and you've got to start all over, warm up the coolness that's come between you, and you can't always do that. But with others, you just pick up where you left off the day, the hour, the minute you saw them last. As if the

21

years that take their toll of everything else have somehow missed a trick. Todd felt that way about seeing Hollis Clarke again. The cloud that hung over him lifted and he was back again on terms with life as it used to be. And it felt good.

He met Hollis Clarke the day he enlisted. He'd been sent for drill to a unit of volunteers, most of them cackhanded rookies like himself. He'd shared a tent with four others. One of them was Hollis. Unlike the rest, Hollis was always at home wherever he went, knew his way around by instinct and, though he was the same age, he treated Todd like a younger brother, looking out for him, showing him the ropes. When their training, such as it was, ended and they moved on, they were assigned to the same platoon. Their regiment was moved up to face the enemy but there was a lot of time for thumb-twiddling while they waited for the generals to decide whether to join battle or wait for a better position, better weather, more reinforcements. Hollis and Todd did a lot of horsing around, a lot of talking, in the course of which they became firm friends. But the fighting could not be put off for ever.

The generals sent regular patrols to spy out the land, hoping to get an edge that would decide the moment to mount an attack. One night, Todd and Hollis, along with half a dozen other men, were ordered out on a sortie. Their mission was to report on enemy movements, but they hadn't been gone twenty minutes when they were caught in open ground by advance Southern scouts. There was a short exchange of gunfire which left all but three of the patrol dead. Two of the survivors dug in under a clump of trees and shot at anything that moved. One was Hollis, the other an Irishman named Keegan who was killed by a bullet in the throat within minutes. Todd, who had got separated from them, kept his head down. When the shooting stopped, he began crawling back to his unit on the far side of the ridge the patrol had crossed. But somehow he got himself turned round in the dark, for suddenly his outstretched hands found space. He dropped a stone but didn't hear it hit bottom. He started backwards but one foot suddenly trod on nothing. He froze, not daring to move until he knew where he was.

Slowly the approaching day pushed the dark out of the sky until he could see that he'd fetched up on a high ledge above a narrow pass. He stood up. Beyond the pass was the enemy line. To his surprise he saw they were breaking camp, dousing fires, taking down tents, harnessing horses. His generals had waited too long: the enemy were about to steal a march on them.

He saw exactly how the move was planned. Instead of hauling up cannon for a bombardment, they were going to march what looked like an entire brigade through the pass. It would take some time — the pass was narrow

— but once they were through, Todd's regiment, taken from the rear, would be dead meat.

He had to get back to base immediately and warn his commanding officer of the danger. He was about to turn and do just that when he realized that the first column of enemy soldiers was already on the move. Even if he got back to his lines in one piece, it would be too late.

The mouth of the pass was too narrow to let more than one mounted cavalryman or two foot soldiers through at a time. He unhooked his cartridge box and counted out his ammunition. Then he loaded his rifle, took aim and waited. He let the first troopers get two or three yards along the narrow trail that snaked between the two rocky walls of the pass, then fired.

In the short time he'd been in the army, he'd become more than a half-decent shot. He got his man with a clean hit in the chest. The others stopped dead, then turned tail and retreated in confusion, leaving the pass empty except for the motionless body of the first man. Todd smiled as he watched them scurry in a panic. From this height, it was like blocking a column of marching ants. He knew that the soldiers were no more likely to be stopped than ants, but he could delay them. He watched for signs of movement in the pass and kept an eye open for snipers who might try to scale the rocks to get a bead on him.

He reloaded.

In the next half hour, enemy officers tried three times to get men through the pass, but each time Todd's rifle stopped the leaders in their tracks and discouraged the rest. But soon he stopped having it all his way. Sharpshooters got into positions where they had him in their sights and he was forced to keep his head down. It was all getting too hot for comfort when he felt a hand tug the left leg of his pants. He turned and saw Hollis:

'What in tarnation are you doing here?'

'I came looking for you, soldier.'

'Good to see you, soldier.'

'I brought some ammo.'

Hollis had heard the shooting and had come to take a peek. He'd brought his cartridge box and Keegan's too. Between them they'd held the pass for three hours and, as the commendation said, saved the regiment from 'almost certain annihilation'. Alerted by the rattle of musketry, their officers had sent up reinforcements and the enemy abandoned their position. From that day on, Todd and Hollis were inseparable. But eventually the twists and turns of the war and the muddle of army life sent them in different directions.

After all the fighting was over, Todd drifted west over the Great Plains as far as the mountains.

'Me?' said Hollis with a grin. 'I rolled around the world, learned bad habits and got into bad ways, the usual story.'

'How'd you find me?'

'Army records. They had Clanton marked down as your last known address. You wrote from there a while back about your discharge, needed a paper for a loan or something. So how have you made out, old friend?'

Todd poured another drink and told him the whole story.

'I'm as sorry as hell to hear about Sarah and your boy. And now this norther's kicked more dirt in your face. Looks like somebody up there don't like you. What'll you do now?'

'First I'm going to get good and drunk,' said Todd, upending the bottle into his glass and waving to the bartender to bring another.

'I'll drink to that,' said Hollis.

And he did. As they talked about the old days, the first bottle gained a brother.

'So what brings you here?' asked Todd.

'I got me a scheme to get rich. I'm tired of being poor, Todd. All my life, I

been taking orders, usually from dumb-
wits who call the shots because they
had the power that goes with money
and authority. It ain't that I want to
order people around, no sir, not my
style. I just don't want to be told what
to do any more.'

Todd nodded: 'It's what I had out on
my place. I was my own man. Me and
Sarah both. Did what we wanted when
we wanted, and whatever it was it was
for us two. It don't take a mint of
money, just proper arranging.'

'Sure, but I don't think that sort of
life would suit me. It was different for
you. You had Sarah. Me, I got nobody.
Except for you, pardner,' he added with
a grin.

Todd grinned back: 'So what's this
plan of yours for cleaning up and
beating John Jacob Astor at his own
millionaire's game?'

'After I quit the army, I couldn't
settle my mind to anything. Married
men had families to go back to when
they got their discharge. But like a lot of

single men, I didn't have roots, nowhere to go back to — one place was just as good or bad as another. I got restless, moved from job to job, staying with it until I got bored or because I stepped out of line and got fired. I worked with cattle, I laid railroad track, set shot in quarries, kept moving on. One day I thought I'd range a mite further. I drifted down to Mexico doing odd jobs on the way, picking up enough Spanish to get by. It ain't the kind of life I'd recommend.

'I fetched up in a bar in a one-horse town named Saissaco and got into a card game. That was one big mistake. I always thought I played a cool poker hand, Todd, but they ate me up. Mind, it would have gone worse for me if I'd won. In those parts, only the home team is allowed to win. They took my money, my gun. I was lucky to keep my pants and boots. The guy I'd gone up against laughed, called me gringo, said he liked the look of me and offered me a job. Said he could use a man like me who spoke English as well as Spanish. Seeing as how the work called for the use of a gun, he let me have mine back. He called it an advance on my first wages. I didn't have much choice. That's how I became one of Escobar's *bandidos*.'

Todd had never heard of Juan Escobar, so Hollis filled in the details. South of the border, he was public enemy number one. He ran a small army of itchy-fingered gunslingers, mostly Mexican but some gringos too. Mainly he robbed banks and kidnapped rich people and demanded large ransoms to release them. But he sometimes stopped trains too and threatened big landowners and cattlemen with all sorts of mayhem unless they paid him to keep away.

'What line of work did you do, Hollis?'

'Most of it was dirty. Escobar is an animal and his men are no better. The rules were simple. Their targets either paid up or got shot, or their families got shot or their houses or businesses got burned down and wrecked.'

'Were you involved in that part of the business? Did you burn any houses down? Did you shoot anybody?'

'At the start I was sent out on a couple of enforcing missions. I took a back seat but I couldn't keep my hands clean altogether. Sure I did things I'm not proud of but, hell, it was do what I was told or get shot myself. Like I said, they weren't sweet persons I was working with.'

Todd said nothing. And, in a world full of so many bad people, Sarah had been taken first!

'You've no cause to look at me that way. I couldn't help myself. You know what they say: needs must when the devil drives.'

The words were like a jab in Todd's ribs; he wondered if he had ever really known Hollis. The Hollis he'd known knew right from wrong and would never had said anything like that.

'And later?' he asked.

'Escobar said he had enough strong-arm men. What he needed was brains. He reckoned I'd be more useful helping him keep track of his operations. He's a very shrewd man but he don't read or write or speak English. So I translated for him, kept records, did basic accounts, that sort of thing. I know more about his business than he does.'

'So how come you're here? If you're his right hand man and know as much as you say, how come he lets you out of his sight?'

'Escobar sent me back to the States to scout out the lie of the land. He's getting big ideas, reckons Mexico's got too small for him. He thinks there's fatter game and richer pickings this side of the border, so he's planning to move here. He's going to leave his brothers to look after the store back home while he forages east and west of the Rockies. To do this he needs financing. He's going to ship a heap of dollars. Soon. We're going to steal it.'

Todd almost spilled his drink.

'Are you serious? You're planning to rob a *bandido* chief who kills as easy as he spits?'

'Why not?' Hollis grinned.

For a split second, Todd saw something around the edges of that grin that didn't used to be there in the old days. The mouth smiled but the eyes weren't laughing. Then the hardness was gone and he thought it must be a trick of the light or the whiskey working or that he must have imagined it.

'I don't know, Hollis. It's a long time since I used a gun. I'm not the same guy you knew. I got soft. I got old. You'd be better off looking for somebody else.'

'At least listen to what I got in mind,' said Hollis, undaunted. 'I need somebody I can trust and there's nobody I trust like I trust you, Todd.'

'Go on, then, and say your piece. But I ain't promising anything.'

'I been playing things cool. Escobar's not just used to having me around, he believes I wouldn't dare double-cross him. I never gave him cause to suspect me of making a move against him and he reckons he pays me too well for me to get ideas. I come and go in his house and he even leaves me alone with Juana. She's his girl just now, but she knows the score too. When he gets tired of her, he'll kick her out if she's lucky, kill her if he's having a bad day. She picked me out, she confides in me. She's sweet but she's also a survivor. Keeps her eyes and ears open, listens at keyholes.'

'Is that as far as you go with her?'

'We've got pretty close,' said Hollis, flashing that same grin. 'But she don't mean any more to me than I do to her. She tells me things. That's how I know exactly how and when Escobar is planning his move to the States. She gives me times and places. Now, listen up. This is how it's going to be.

'Escobar has got a lot of dollars together. Juana reckons it's not less than ten thousand and could be as much as twenty. In six days' time, he'll fill three, maybe four or more leather bags depending on the size of his stash, and ride with an escort to the border and over it, as far as Campo Largo. I'm to meet him there, stay with him and put him wise to what I scouted out — towns with banks, which big ranchers have daughters to kidnap, which trains have regular pay-loads and when. We'll take the stage east out of Campo on the second of next month, or maybe a day later. I've told him trailside robbers and Indians ain't a problem, not with the Texas Rangers keeping the lid closed down tight on such things. He'll travel as a business-man and have his money with him. We'll head for Roper's Fork — I'll tell him that's where I found just the place for him to set up in.'

'Will it be just you and him in the coach?'

'Nope. He'll have at least a couple of bodyguards. Now, there's a hill . . . '

'Any chance of bribing the body-guards? It would make life a lot easier if they were on side.'

'See?' said Hollis, rubbing his hands. 'You ain't such a slouch after all, asking the right questions. Juana thinks it's possible. She's working on it. But like I was saying, this hill. When the coach gets to the top, you'll be waiting there with a spare horse for me.'

'You want me to step into the road and rob the coach?'

'Nope. By then I'll have a gun in Escobar's ribs. As long as it's there his men won't dare make a move if they're still loyal, and won't anyway if they're not. You'll keep a gun on them while they toss the bags down, then you'll hitch the bags on the saddles. By then I'll have Escobar trussed up like a chicken. We cut the traces and whack the coach horses so they take off, that way Escobar's left with no way of coming after us. We mount up and ride off into the sunset, leaving them stranded.'

Todd considered the plan. It was well enough thought out; it might just work.

'It's stealing,' he said. 'In the old days

you bent rules but stealing wasn't your style.'

'That was in another life, Todd. I've seen a lot of things that ain't my style, and done some of 'em too. I know what makes the world go round and it sure ain't preachers' rules. Think a minute. How can you steal from a thief?'

'But stolen money still wouldn't belong to you.'

'And who would it belong to, Todd? Who would you give it back to? To all the people it was stolen from? How would you know who they were? Or where they are? Or whether they were exaggerating the amounts Escobar had squeezed off them? How would you even it all up in a way that satisfied your conscience? No, stolen money belongs to whoever takes it from the thief. If you think it's dirty, you could always make it clean again by doing good with it. A dollar ain't good or bad, it's just paper or metal. But one thing's for sure, as long as all that money's in Escobar's pocket, he won't be using it to do anybody any good except himself.'

Todd wondered how a wrong could be bent so far that it made a right, but for the moment couldn't think of a way of answering Hollis. Anyway, maybe his friend was on to something. What good had doing the right thing, going by preachers' rules, done for him? Maybe it was time to get wise and get his finger in the pie.

'All right, count me in,' he said. 'But what about Juana? Are you sure of her? Or is she stringing you along? Maybe it's a test set up by Escobar to see how far he can trust you.'

'She's straight, no fear on that score. She gets a cut. I say we split fifty for me, forty for you and ten for her of whatever the haul is. She has a brother in Campo Largo, she wants me to get her share to him. He'll see she gets it later. All right? Got any more questions?

'Sure. If Escobar's the mean *hombre* you make out, won't he be good and mad? Won't he do everything he can to get his money back and put a bullet through your head and mine too? He'll come after us and won't give up till he's got even.'

'No chance,' said Hollis. 'We'll leave him there spitting cobs on the top of that hill with no gun, no horse and no way of knowing which way we've gone. Todd, we'll put so much distance between us and him he'll never trace us. We'll be over the hills and far away and he won't be able to do a damn thing about it. This is a big, big country.'

Todd fell silent. But think as hard as he could, he couldn't come up with a good reason not to throw in with his old army buddy.

So what if it was stealing? Little Phil, Sarah, the norther: it didn't look as if playing it straight, going by the book, had earned him any marks for good behaviour. He was angry at the sky, the world, the whiskey he was drinking, at everything.

He lifted his glass and said: 'When do we start?'

3

Hold Up

Ten days later, Todd Coulter was sitting on a rock on top of a hill half a day's coach ride from Roper's Fork. His horse was tethered in a stand of mesquite back of the rock. Beside it was the grey mare Hollis had picked out from Hank Beynon's stables thirty miles back in Clanton, a place Todd confidently never expected to see again.

He took out the makings and rolled himself a smoke. As he lit it, he took another long hard look down the hill, down over the plain that stretched into the blue-hazed distance. The now familiar view was as empty as a politician's promises. Nothing moved that wasn't a wind devil or a ball of tumbleweed.

Hollis had chosen the spot well for an ambush. By the time the stage was nearing the top, the horses would be blowing, slowing almost to a stop as they looked forward to their regular breather. Hollis said the coach always halted here to let the horses get their wind back. Also, the cover was good. Todd could wait until the last minute before stepping out from behind his rock on to the trail, waving his gun at the driver and telling him to stop. But if the place was right, the time was all wrong.

Hollis had gone off to meet up with Escobar in Campo Largo as arranged. There they were supposed to take the stage the next day, the second of July, or maybe a day later. It was now the seventh and no coach had come by in the interval. Todd knew it didn't run everyday. But he couldn't come up with any good reason to say why he hadn't seen hide nor hair of anything that looked like a stage. A cart or two had passed and the occasional lone rider.

He was sure he'd got the right hill — Hollis's directions had been clear. Maybe the coach was still in Roper's Fork with a busted axle or was waiting for a new wheel. Maybe there'd been border trouble and the army had requisitioned the horses.

But it could also be that all bets were off. Maybe Hollis had run into trouble. Maybe Escobar had rumbled him. Maybe Juana had talked. Maybe even Hollis was dead. Maybe all sorts. With the way Todd's luck was running these days, that could well have happened.

He'd left Clanton on the first of the month as agreed and found the dell Hollis had told him about. It was a couple of hundred yards further down the other side of the hill and well hidden from the road. It had a spring and grazing for the horses. He set up a temporary camp there and sat down to wait.

But now his supplies were running out — he had enough tobacco but food only for another day — as was his patience.

43

He flicked the end of his cigarette into the dust where it went smoking for a minute before burning itself out. He shifted his position and tilted his hat further down over his forehead. The sweat trickled into his eyes, making him blink. He blinked again, then jerked upright. In the distance something was raising a cloud of dust and it wasn't no wind or tumbleweed. He got off the rock as if it had just started burning holes in the seat of his pants; he didn't want to be skylined, though the coach was still too far away for there to be much danger of that. But if Escobar's bodyguards were sharp, and Escobar's money could buy the sharpest, there was no sense in taking chances of giving his position away.

From the cover of his rock, Todd followed the progress of the coach. At first it seemed to make little impression on the distance it had to cover. But slowly it ate up the miles. It moved steadily along the trail and then slowed as it began its ascent. The nearer it got, the slower it came. First Todd heard the rumble of the wheels, then the hollering of the driver, the jingle of the harness and the snorting of the horses. When it was a hundred yards below him, toiling now, with the driver laying on with the whip and the horses almost winded, Todd checked his gun one last time. When the rig was no more than twenty yards away and almost slowed to a stop, he stepped out from his rock and loosed off a shot into the air.

'Hold it there!' he barked.

The driver reined in. He'd never been held up before and for a moment thought here was a traveller stopping the coach because he was in trouble, maybe with a horse that had broken a leg or cast a shoe, and was wanting a ride. He soon realized how wrong he was when Todd kept his six-gun up and ordered the guard riding shotgun to throw down his weapon. Almost simultaneously there was a shot inside the coach. The arrangement was that as soon as Todd stopped the rig, Hollis would get the drop on Escobar and his bodyguards too who, if Juana had failed to buy them off, would try to do their job. The shot told Todd that Juana hadn't managed it and Escobar's men were not on side. A moment later the door of the coach opened.

A heavy-set man of forty or so stepped down on to the trail. Todd raised his Colt, cocked it and kept it pointing at him. It had to be Escobar. His face was dark with anger. He was followed by a second man, younger, lighter, with fancy pants and a black leather waistcoat studded with silver. He had both hands in the air and no gun in his holster. Then a body was pushed out. It belonged to what might have been the brother of the Mexicano in the fancy pants. There was blood on the front of his shirt and his gun was still holstered, but it didn't look as if he'd be using it any time soon, if ever. Then Hollis stepped out and closed the door behind him. He looked back briefly and said reassuringly through the window to the other passengers in the coach:

'Sorry for the inconvenience, to you ma'am, and you, sir and you, Reverend. There's no cause for you folks to be alarmed. We'll be on our way in just a moment, though you might have to stay here a spell.'

Todd told Escobar and his bodyguard to throw their guns down and kept his Colt pointing at them. Hollis called to the man riding shotgun to toss down the four leather satchels they were carrying on the roof. When the last of the bags thudded on to the trail, he took over from Todd and kept the Mexicanos covered while Todd got the horses and slung the bags over the pommels of their saddles. Next he cut the coach's traces and freed the horses which, for all that they were weary and weak-legged after toiling up the hill, ran off in a panic when he waved his hat at them, whooped and whacked them on the rump.

Escobar recovered from the shock and a stream of venom poured from a mouth which had too many teeth and was edged by a heavy gaucho moustache. Todd didn't understand a word but he didn't need to. He got the man's meaning easy: he wasn't wishing anybody happy birthday or a long life. Todd got on his horse and kept his gun on the two *bandidos* while Hollis swung up into the saddle. For a moment, he looked down at Escobar.

'*Muchas gracias, compañero*. Nice doing business with you. But I won't say *hasta la vista* . . .'

Then he turned his horse and dug his heels into its ribs.

Todd was about to do the same when he caught a movement out of the corner of his eye. He shouted a warning, drew his gun and fired, but it was too late. Todd cursed himself for being careless. The *bandido* Hollis had shot in the coach wasn't as dead as he'd seemed. He had worked his gun into his hand and got in a couple of quick shots before Todd's first bullet got him again. The second and third made Escobar and his sidekick scatter and dive for cover. Then he wheeled his horse and took off fast after Hollis.

Hollis was already fifty yards away and going fast, but fast in a way that gave Todd the odd feeling that the speed was down to his horse running away with him. He dug hard with his spurs but it took him the best part of a mile to catch up. By this time, Hollis's horse, which had been spooked by the gunshots and had bolted, was slowing and responding to some pretty weak pressure on the reins. Todd soon saw why Hollis didn't seem in charge.

There was a patch of blood high on his right shoulder: he'd been hit.

Todd drew alongside.

'How bad is it?' he yelled.

But he needn't have asked. The front of Hollis's shirt gleamed wet and red. If the slug had made a clean entry near the shoulder blade it had left a mess on the way out.

'There were two shots. What happened to the other?'

'Musta gone wide,' mouthed Hollis. His face was grey under his heavy tan and his mouth was slack.

'Slow down, so we can take a look and see how bad it is.'

But Hollis shook his head: 'Got to stick with the plan,' he muttered through gritted teeth.

They'd agreed they'd stay on the trail for as long as they were visible from the top of the hill where Escobar would be watching and cursing them. Only when they rounded the bluff that rose out of the plain still a couple of miles further along the main trail would they turn north. They'd cover their tracks so Escobar would have no idea which way they'd gone. The plan was to disappear, to lose themselves in the desert. That way, they'd keep the money they'd stolen.

They rode on. The grey was now responding to the rein Hollis held in his left hand. He had little control over his right arm which swung with the motions of the horse and was clearly giving him a lot of pain. Todd hoped he wasn't going to pass out. With a wound like that, he was amazed that his friend was still in the saddle.

After what seemed like an hour but couldn't have been more than a few minutes, they rounded the bluff. Todd looked back to check. They could no longer be seen from the hill.

'Time to turn off,' growled Hollis in a voice Todd scarcely recognized.

They turned left off the trail. Leaving Hollis to go on alone, Todd got down, broke off a branch of sage and swept the place where they'd left the trail. Then he took off after Hollis and caught him up after a quarter of a mile or so. The grey mare had slowed to not much more than a gentle amble.

Todd leaned over his horse's neck, reached out and brought the grey to a stop. It was still blowing hard and its eyes were flecked red with wildness, but it stood quietly enough in the middle of the trail. Now that he was no longer bracing himself against the movement,

Hollis started to sway. He grabbed his pommel with his good hand; his grip on it was the only thing that prevented him from falling off.

Todd dismounted and helped his friend down. When he had got him in the shade of a stand of cottonwood, he took a look at the wound. What he saw was bad news.

The bullet had entered just over Hollis's right shoulder-blade. It must have nicked a bone and tumbled, so that when it came out of his chest it was side on and tore a gaping wound. If it was a good thing the slug had gone straight through, the amount of blood Hollis had lost and was continuing to lose had already sapped his strength. The wound needed to be bound to stop the flow. Todd cast round for something he could use as a bandage, but men who set out to rob a Mexican *bandido* don't take no medical kit with them. He fetched his water bottle and slopped water over the angry, raw-edged hole. With his knife, he cut Hollis's shirt away, salvaged the part of it that was still clean and balled it into a pad which he placed over the tear in his chest. He told Hollis to hold it there, partly because it needed holding but also because he didn't want him passing out. Giving him something to do would keep him conscious. He wished he had a bottle of whiskey — they both could do with a shot. He took off his own shirt and tore out the sleeves. With one he tied the pad in place and used the other as a sling which took the weight of that more or less useless right arm.

'Thanks, soldier. That feels a lot better.'

Todd gave him a drink of water. Slowly the colour was returning to his friend's face.

'So what happened?'

'Juana's dead. Escobar found out about her. She thought she'd bribed one of his bodyguards, Paco, not the one with the fancy outfit.'

'The one you shot.'

'That's him. Anyway, Paco seemed to

go along with it but he reported straight back to his boss. One night, the three of us were sitting over a glass of tequila. Escobar suddenly came out with it, wanted to know why she was offering money to one of his boys, asked where she got it from, what she was up to. He didn't wait for answers. He just reached for his gun and shot her. Through the head.'

'He still didn't suspect you?'

'He suspects everybody. I tell you, friend, I had to do some quick thinking. But I talked my way out of it.'

'So when I stopped the coach,' said Todd, 'one of his boys went for his gun and you beat him to the draw?'

'Sure did. I knew there'd be shooting, so I was ready for it. Made the most of my advantage.'

'All that's history,' said Todd. 'We're not out of this yet. We've got a start on Escobar. We've got something to ride and he hasn't. But we got to get going if we're to keep ahead of him. You feel up to riding yet?'

'No choice. We got to put a lot of miles between us and him. If there are any horses anywhere roundabouts, he'll get his hands on them. He's not the sort that gives up easy. He'll come after us because, guess what we stole? Near twenty thousand!'

Todd managed a grin but money was the last thing on his mind. He was thinking of the carts and riders who had passed him while he'd been sitting on his rock. It would be a big mistake to count on Escobar staying stranded on top of that hill for long.

'So what are we waiting for?'

Todd brought the grey mare and helped Hollis into the saddle. The effort made him pant and the colour that had crept back into his face drained away again, leaving him looking ashen. Todd set a steady pace.

He'd seen enough war wounds to know what Hollis was feeling. There were good and bad wounds. Some disabled a man, made him unfit to fight, gave him a lot of pain, but didn't threaten life or limb. With that kind of wound, a soldier was on an easy ticket. He got sent to a field dressing station or maybe got dispatched back far behind the lines, for treatment in a hospital, away from the fighting. But there were other kinds of wounds which did damage to vital parts. They didn't always look as if they could kill, but they often did. Todd didn't like the look of the hit Hollis had taken.

After an hour's easy riding, they'd made five or six miles. They'd just crested a rise and Todd called a halt. He dismounted and looked back the way they'd come. No one was following them.

He helped Hollis dismount. He was still weak but he could have been in worse shape. Still, there was sweat beading his forehead. Why shouldn't there be? The heat had yet to go out of the day and when it's hot, people sweat. But this was somehow different. There was something feverish about his old friend.

'How am I doing, soldier?' asked Hollis.

'You're doing fine for now. But that's a nasty wound you got there. I reckon you've got a touch of fever. Could be the shock of the hit you took. But we can't afford for the wound to get infected. You need a doctor, Hollis, and soon. So come on. Sit there any longer and you'll get too stiff to move.'

'Sooner or later we all get stiff permanent and then we stop moving for good and all and ever and ever.'

'Now ain't that a cheerful thought. But it ain't your time just yet, soldier. So come on, shake a leg.'

4

Sanctuary

If everything had gone according to plan, they should by now have been forty or fifty miles south of the hill where they'd taken Escobar's money away from him. But by Todd's reckoning they were now no more than twenty or so miles from Clanton, a place he thought he'd seen the back of. It was not just the obvious place to find help, it was the only place for more miles than Hollis was capable of riding in his shot-up state. Even twenty miles would be a tall order.

By sundown they'd covered maybe fifteen of the twenty. They kept stopping for Hollis to rest. The bleeding had started again and loss of blood was making him feverish.

'Keep thinking about the money, Hollis. You can't let an itty-bitty bullet get in the way of you and all that cash. Think of the cigars, the steaks, the girls!'

'Lemme see some of it,' said Hollis. 'Lemme hold it and smell it.'

Todd reached into one of the bags, brought out a tight packet of dollar bills, broke into it and passed a few of them over.

While Hollis held them, ran them through his fingers, stroked them, loved them, Todd rolled them each a cigarette and, with one of the bills he gave Hollis a light.

'I always wanted to do that,' he said, dropping the ashes on to the trail.

Hollis grinned.

'That's it, pardner,' said Todd. 'Just keep thinking about the money! It ain't pieces of paper you got there, it's the colour and shape of the rest of your life. You're rich, so don't you forget it!'

The thought was enough to get Hollis to sit up in the saddle and good for another couple of miles.

It was getting dark when Todd, who was leading Hollis's horse by the reins, made out a heavier patch of gloom off the trail in the growing shadows. It proved to be a clump of trees which hid a small creek with water in it. He decided to hole up there. Maybe a night's rest would give Hollis enough of his strength back to ride on in the morning as planned. They used the bags full of their money for pillows, but though it was the stuff of dreams it wasn't made for resting heads on and neither of them got much sleep. As soon as the sky began showing signs of the new day, Todd was up and about.

He fetched water from the creek in his hat, wiped the fever sweat off Hollis, made him drink as much as he could take and refilled both their canteens. He washed out the compress he'd put on the wound which now looked dark red and angry, and replaced it. It was the best he could do. He had nothing else to use. There was no point in even thinking about breakfast. They had no supplies and they couldn't risk a shot at a jackrabbit that might attract unwanted attention. Because one thing was for sure: Escobar was not going to give up on them.

Todd hadn't got much shuteye but at least he'd had time to think.

'Listen, Hollis. If we're going to stay ahead of Escobar and his boys, we should be aiming to go anywhere except Clanton. It's the first place they'll start looking to pick up our trail. There's no other towns, so that's where they'll go. But you're in bad shape so getting a doctor has got to be top of your list of things to do today. Even comes before vanishing into the blue yonder without leaving a trace. But, shot up the way you are, it's got to be Clanton. Ain't no place else.'

'Escobar must know I was hit. If Clanton's the first place he'll look, the first door he knocks on will be the doc's.'

'We got no choice.'

'Sure. But that don't mean we got to ride down the main street with a sign on our hats with our names on. Ain't there some place out of town where we can hole up? You could ride into town and fetch the doc back. You could stock up with supplies so we needn't ever show our faces. What about that farm of yours you told me about?'

'Naw,' said Todd as they ambled along. 'It got too beat up by the norther. Ain't enough left standing to give shelter for a gopher.'

He thought of Mick Murphy who'd be glad to help. Mick was a good friend but he wasn't a fighting man. Todd didn't want to drag him into this. Besides, the fewer people who knew where they were the safer they'd be. What they needed was a hideaway where Hollis could be put back together in one piece, and for that he needed a doctor.

'Maybe we could use Ben Smiley's place.'

'Who's he?'

'A loner. Tried his hand at farming but he wasn't suited to it. Anyway, he wasn't the settling sort, more a wandering man. A couple or three years back he just drifted away west one day. Nobody's heard tell of him since. It's a few miles outside town. Nobody much ever goes out that way.'

'Sounds as safe as the bosom of Abraham,' said Hollis with a weak grin.

Their progress was even slower than on the previous day and the stops were more frequent. But there wasn't as far to go. They got to the Smiley smallholding by early after-noon. The cabin was derelict but it had everything they needed, including a well that wasn't silted up. Hollis was done in. Todd found a bed with a mattress still on it and helped him get comfortable. There was too much of the day left to do much yet about the main business, which was to go fetch Doc Halpern. Like Hollis had said, it would be tempting fate to ride into Clanton while it was still light and show his face for all to see.

'I'll take off just before sundown,' said Todd, 'so it'll be dark by the time I get there.'

'What about the money?' said Hollis weakly. 'You ain't figuring on leaving it lying around for anybody passing by to pick up while you're away? I couldn't stop them. It's more than I can do to sit up straight.'

'There's nobody passes by. I told you. The money'll be fine here, on the table, so you won't forget to think about it.'

He had brought the saddle bags into the house when he'd seen to the horses. Then he noticed Hollis was asleep. Todd didn't like the way he slipped in and out of consciousness. The sooner he got Doc Halpern on the case, the better.

He sat for a moment and thought about what Hollis had said about hiding the money. Maybe he was right. Anyway, he couldn't set off for a spell so he might as well use the time to put it somewhere out of sight.

He scouted round the farm. Some of the outbuildings had not survived as well as the main house, and their roofs had fallen in, but one barn was still in reasonable shape and more than sound enough for the purpose. He found a shovel and dug a hole in one corner of the barn floor. He dropped the bags containing the money into it. They were heavy. He paused, opened one and took out the packet he'd broken open for Hollis to see. He took out enough bills to cover immediate expenses, and slipped them into his pants' pocket. Then he closed the bag, put it back in the hole with the others, covered all four with the earth he had dug out and laid half a dozen fencing posts over the newly dug earth, casually, as camouflage. Then he went out and shot them some supper. He gathered wood for the stove and roasted the rabbits that had moved in after Smiley had moved out.

Hollis managed to get some food inside him and rallied a mite. 'Where's the money?' he asked suddenly.

'Safe.'

'Yeah, but where's it at? What you do with it? It's best we both know where it is. That way if one of us goes down, it ain't lost altogether.'

'There's no need to worry,' said Todd.

'I ain't worrying. I just want to know where it is. It ain't a secret. You gonna tell me?'

'All right, all right,' said Todd, half irritated by what Hollis seemed to be implying. 'I buried it in the barn. There's some fencing posts marking the place.'

'You count it?'

'Nope. No time. Anyway it's best we do it together, so all is clear and in the open. We'll do it tomorrow. You'll be feeling better then after the doc's looked you over.'

'How heavy did the bags feel? Did they feel like they had twenty thousand inside them?'

'Hard to judge, Hollis. I never had

twenty thousand dollars in a bag before. But however much is there, it's surprising how a round sum of dollars can weigh.'

'We should count it now. That way there'd be no room for mistakes and misunderstandings. You got to be very careful with money, Todd. It has a way of coming between friends and setting families at each others' throats.'

Hollis's meaning was clear. While he'd been lying in his cot, all passed out, Todd had had all the time in the world to cream off some of the pickings for himself.

'It's all there, Hollis,' Todd said quietly. 'I ain't touched a penny of it, except about thirty dollars I filched that I'll need to pay the doc and buy supplies in town. Is that all right with you?'

'Sure,' said Hollis. 'I believe you. Why wouldn't I?'

'You're not thinking straight, old friend. Listen to me. Counting it isn't top of the list of important things to do.

Number one job is fetching the doc.'

'You're right. Sorry. We'll count it later. Divide it up, split it fifty, forty and ten.'

'Is Juana's ten per cent still part of the deal?'

'Damn. I forgot. Juana's out of it. We'll split her ten per cent between us.'

'No, Hollis. This was your set-up. You have it. I'll be happy with a sixty-forty split.'

Hollis looked at him suspiciously for a moment, then relaxed and closed his eyes.

'One more job to do,' said Todd. 'We got to cook up a story for the doc. We need a yarn to account for how you got shot in the back. You couldn't have done it yourself, so it warn't no accident.'

'*Bandidos*,' said Hollis through half-closed eyes.

'We got stopped on the road. They shot at us. We shot back. Two of theirs was killed and I got a slug in the shoulder. That all right?'

'Right, *bandidos* it is,' said Todd. 'Sun's almost down, time to go. Anything else you need?'

The answer was a snore. Hollis had passed out again. His breathing was irregular and sweat stood out on his skin like a rash of blisters.

Todd saddled up and rode into town. The moon was up, under the stars, the land looked like it was made of silver.

As he rode, an odd thought crossed his mind. Could it be that Hollis was shamming? That he wasn't in such a bad way as he made out? Would he still be in Smiley's bed when I get back, he thought, or will he take the money and get out while I'm gone? Almost immediately he pushed the thought out of his mind as unworthy. Hollis was the best friend he'd ever had. Friends don't behave like that.

But Hollis was right about one thing. Money, especially a large quantity of it, can make waves in the stillest pool.

He tethered his horse in bushes on the edge of town. Pulling his hat well down over his face so no one would recognize him, he headed for Doc Halpern's house, keeping to the shadows and ducking into doorways when he heard anyone coming.

The doc himself answered his knock. He was surprised to see him because Todd had made a point of telling him goodbye and saying he was going away for good. Todd slipped quickly inside the door and cut short the chit-chat. He explained he had a wounded man holed up in the cabin on Ben Smiley's old place. He'd have taken him home, but he didn't have a home since the norther had flattened it. A friend, he said, an old army pal. Was hurt very bad. Gunshot wound.

'It ain't like you to get mixed up in shoot-outs, Todd,' said the doctor, raising an eyebrow.

'Save the questions till later, Doc. Hollis has lost a lot of blood. I think the wound's infected. Sometimes you're talking to him and he just passes out. I don't think he's in his head some of the time.'

'I'll get my bag.'

'I'll catch you up on the road,' said Todd. 'I need to get some supplies from the stores.'

'Don't forget whiskey, I'll need something to disinfect the wound with. Make it a couple of bottles. And get some cotton cloth for bandages.'

Later, out on the silver road, Todd caught up with the doc, tossed his bag of supplies into the back of the buggy and trotted alongside.

'Your friend . . . what was his name again?'

'Hollis. We served in the same regiment. We're like brothers. I don't see him for years and then he just turns up out of the blue. Came at the right time. Same day as the norther . . . '

After a moment, the doc went on: 'Your friend got shot, you said. How did that happen?'

'*Bandidos*. We were out on the road to Roper's Fork. I figure the Mexes had crossed the border on a raid. We were unlucky and got in their way.'

'What happened?'

'They tried a stick up but they weren't much good at it. We got a couple of shots in first and then there was a shoot-out. We got two of them but Hollis took a hit in the right shoulder. Bullet went through but made a bigger hole on the way out than it had on the way in.'

Doc Halpern seemed to believe the story. There was no reason why he shouldn't.

When they reached Smiley's cabin, Hollis was still noisily asleep. Todd lit some of the candles he'd bought and helped the doc sit the wounded man up in his cot. At first, Hollis didn't know where he was. He rolled his eyes and tried to speak but no words came out. The doc talked to him, made him drink some water, then held a smelling bottle under his nose. Hollis's eyes focused and he grinned.

'You must be the doc, Todd's good friend,' he said.

'Give me the whiskey,' said the doc

and he poured a good slug of it down Hollis's throat straight from the neck of the bottle.

He handed it back to Todd and said: 'When I say so, give him some more. He'll need it. What I've got to do is going to hurt. Meantime, go fetch water.'

He told Hollis to lean forward while he undid the makeshift bandage and compress Todd had tended the wound with. He held a candle over Hollis's back and peered at the entry wound.

'That don't look too bad.'

He told Hollis to lie back again and took a much longer look at the hole on the right side of his chest.

'Your friend reckoned you've got some infection there. Well, your friend was right. Here, take another slug of whiskey while I think. More. More again.'

Todd came back with the water: 'Well?'

The doc washed the wound so he could get a better idea of the extent of the damage.

'It don't look good. The bullet went in, clipped a bone, rolled and came out wrong. That ain't all bad, because at least it came out. But I reckon it took something in with it, a piece of shirt most like, and it's still in there. That's what's causing the infection. I'm going to have to fish it out. If I don't, our boy don't stand a chance. Give him another drink. I want him to finish the bottle. Then I'll go into that hole in his chest, poke around and see what I can find. If he hasn't passed out by then, I'll need you to hold him down.'

'Am I goin' to be hokay?' asked Hollis. 'I mean, will I s'ill be able to git up on a norse and shoo' Mexes withou' the 'sistance of my goo' fren' Todd Coulter here pres'nt?'

'No reason why not, provided I can clean out the wound and stop the infection. It's going to hurt some, so don't tell me afterwards I never warned you.'

They sat smoking while Hollis finished the bottle and his speech grew

74

more slurred. Todd knew he had a larger capacity than a single bottle. But he was in bad shape and his tolerance was low. Suddenly he stopped talking, closed his eyes and went slack.

Immediately Doc Halpern rolled up his sleeves and told Todd to bring all the candles he had so that he had light to see by.

An hour later, the wound was clean, fresh dressings and bandages had been applied and Doc Halpern was sipping at a tin mug, one of old Ben's that he'd left behind, full of hot coffee.

'He'll be fine. We were just in time. The infection was just starting to take off, but I reckon we've caught it. He'll need some rest and feeding up, though. Your boy's lost a lot of blood, so he'll be below par for a couple of weeks.'

'Thanks, Doc. How much do I owe you?'

'Don't worry about that. Between friends . . . '

'Mighty good of you but we've got money to pay,' is what Todd said but inwardly he was thinking: 'more money than you've seen in your whole damn life or ever will!'

'As you like. A straight ten dollars all right?'

Todd extracted ten singles from his pants' pocket and handed them over.

Doc Halpern said that was fine and took the money.

'It was just as well your friend showed up when he did,' he said. 'We all thought you were ready to give up. When you decided to take off and go looking for fame and fortune someplace else, we were all happy. You had no reason to stay in this neck of the woods. Too many bad things happened here. Too many memories.'

The old man scratched his head.

'But I still can't figure it out. You took off a week ago but you ain't got very far. And how come you fetched up here, off the beaten track, when you could have ridden a couple more miles and got your friend a comfortable billet in town?'

'I told you, we were shot at on the Draper's Fork road,' said Todd coolly. 'We headed back because Clanton was nearest. We were damned lucky to get this far, Doc. The way Hollis was, he couldn't have ridden ten yards further. I was just about holding him on his horse.'

'Fair enough,' said the doc, getting to his feet. 'Any of that whiskey left? I'll take a snort before I go. I'll stop by tomorrow, see how the patient's doing. He's sleeping now and looks like the fever's going down. He'll be fine.'

After the doc had gone, Todd took off his boots and sat in Ben Smiley's chair. He was dead beat but sleep wouldn't come. For the moment, everything was panning out fine. But something nagged at the back of his mind. It went on nagging and finally Todd knew what was worrying him.

'I need to get free of Hollis as soon as soon. We got to go our separate ways. Escobar only saw me for a couple of minutes and he wouldn't have been paying me much attention anyway what with everything else that was going on. If he saw me again, he probably wouldn't know me from a bird in a tree. But Hollis was real close to him for months. Hollis could grow a moustache and wear a black coat and Escobar would still be able to pick him out of a crowd of preachers. The longer I stay with Hollis, the more dangerous it is for me. Hollis is the one he wants and he won't stop until he's got him. I'd be a lot safer on my own. I got to get out!'

He decided he would dig up the money, take his half and get out of there.

But how would he live with himself afterwards? Hollis was his friend. Hollis was sick. No way could he walk out on him while he was helpless. He was still arguing with himself when he fell asleep.

Hollis woke first. The sun was up.

'Call me Jonah,' he said.

Todd opened his eyes: 'How d'you feel?'

'Like I was run over by a herd of buffalo. And I got a hangover I'd willingly trade for half of my half of the money you buried in the barn. See, I remember things.'

While Todd lit the stove and got the coffee going and set the flapjacks to warm, Hollis stretched, moved his right arm gingerly and winced.

'The doc said he'd be round today, see how you're getting on.'

'You known him long? Do you trust him?'

'Like I trust you, pal,' said Todd.

'Which is how far?'

'All the way so far,' said Todd. 'I looked after you good, Hollis. I didn't leave you at the creek we stopped at, though I could have. You were weak as a kitten. I could have taken your gun off you and ridden away with all the money. But I didn't.'

'Does that mean you thought about it? Or maybe you've been sitting here thinking about it while I was off in whiskeyland?'

'Friends don't double-cross each other. You need me till you're fit and well and you know you can count on me being here for you. But there's something I've been giving thought to. I don't think Escobar would recognize me, but he's coming after you and, from what you've told me, he's a determined son of a bitch. If I stay close to you, looking out for you the way I said, I'm putting myself at risk. Now risk comes expensive. A man gets more money for taking a risk.'

'What are you saying, Todd?'

'If I stay I want the split to be fifty fifty.'

Hollis Clarke stared at his friend, then shrugged his shoulders.

'Fair enough. But neither of us knows what we each have got fifty percent of. When we've done eating, go get the bags and we'll count the money. We could both do with some cheering up.'

5

Doubts and Fears

Todd opened the bags one by one and shook the contents on to the chair he'd slept in the night before. They formed a pyramid. Not a large one — a large sum of money doesn't take up a lot of space.

The money was all in notes, done up in bundles. Each bundle was held by a paper wrapper. The last three bundles fell off the pyramid and hit the floor with a light thud. Paper doesn't weigh enough to make a hullabaloo.

Todd bent down and picked them up, put one back on the heap, handed one to Hollis and kept one for himself. Hollis stared at his, weighed it in his hand. Todd riffled through the bills that peeked out of one end.

'What you got there, pardner?' he

said. 'I got me a bundle of singles.'

Hollis said: 'I guess we made it, pardner. Seeing that goodly pile on the chair and having one of these in my hand gives me a warm feeling, like I was a kid holding a puppy. Mine is all five dollar bills.'

'How many you reckon there are in a bundle?'

They started counting. Hollis's right hand wasn't much use and the fingers of his left fumbled so much that he was obliged to start again.

'I got a hundred bills in mine,' said Todd.

A few minutes later, Hollis said: 'Me too.'

They both paused and looked at the pile.

'Guess what,' said Hollis, 'I got me $500 dollars here in my hand. I never saw so much money at one time in my whole life.'

'And I got a straight hundred,' said Todd. 'Hollis: we're rich!'

Hollis began a whoop but stopped

when the celebration made him move his arm and the pain of it hit him. Todd whooped twice as hard to make up for it. He washed his face with the bundles. He clasped an armful to his chest and hugged them. He spread them out on the floor and rolled on them, kicking his legs in the air.

After a while, Hollis said: 'So how much exactly did we get?'

'Only one way to find out,' said Todd, getting to his feet. 'Let's count it.'

He passed two handfuls of bundles to Hollis who arranged them in piles on his bed.

'I got ones, fives and tens. They all look about the same size as the ones we counted out so I guess they're all bundles of one hundred.'

Todd also put his in neat piles. Suddenly he cried:

'Look what I got here: a bundle of twenties! That's $2,000 in one packet. That's some rich bundle!'

'Let's have a drink,' said Hollis. 'All this counting is thirsty work.'

Todd poured them a slug of whiskey apiece and they started putting the bundles in separate piles by denomination.

When they'd done, they totalled the count. There were exactly a hundred bundles of one dollar bills, eight of fives, four of tens, one of twenties and one thinner bundle of assorted notes made up of thirteen fives and thirty-nine ones, which made $104.

'So that makes, all in all,' said Todd, 'twenty thousand one hundred and four dollars!'

'Gimme another drink,' said Hollis, 'I need it. Jeez, Todd, we struck Yukon gold here!'

'We split it fifty-fifty, right?' said Todd.

'Like we agreed. That makes $10,000 apiece . . . '

' . . . plus the small change.'

They looked at each other and burst out laughing. Suddenly Todd sobered up, cocked his head and said:

'Somebody coming.'

He sprang to his feet, scattering the bundles he had counted in his lap and crossed quickly to the window and looked out.

'It's all right,' he said. 'It's only Doc Halpern. He said he'd be back to see how you're doing. But we'd best get the money out of sight. It would be hard explaining how we came by all this cash.'

He looked round for a suitable place to hide the money. There was hardly any furniture in the room, and no press or cupboards big enough to stash the 114 bundles of Escobar's money.

'Under the bed,' said Hollis. 'And make it fast!'

Todd gathered up the bundles he had dropped and, taking the pile from Hollis's blanket, pushed them with his foot under the cot. What a way to treat money, he thought. He checked to see they were all well out of sight then walked out the door on to the stoop to greet the doc.

'How's your boy this morning?' said Halpern. 'I mean apart from the hangover,' he added with a grin.

'He snored like a warthog, kept me awake half the night,' said Todd, responding in kind, 'and then ate his breakfast like he'd never seen breakfast before. He's just fine, Doc. Thanks to you,' he added, less because it was true, which it was, than because he wanted to keep the doc happy so that he wouldn't stay long. With all that money lying around, it wasn't a good idea to have strangers about the place.

'Let's see the patient,' said the doc and he led the way in.

He gave Hollis a good looking over, put a fresh dressing over the wound and told him to keep the arm still for a couple of days and go easy on it for at least a month after that. Eventually he'd be as good as new.

'Fit young feller like you can shrug off little things like getting shot. You're out of the woods,' he said, closing his bag and standing up.

'You want some coffee?' said Todd, to be polite.

'Thank you, no. I have some visits to make. Mrs Chamberlain's baby's due about now, it'll be her twelfth, and Tom Fielding fell off a barn roof last week. Broke his leg, got himself a nasty fracture. So I'll be on my way. Anyway, Mrs Chamberlain's coffee is bound to be an improvement on yours.'

'Will you need to come again?' asked Todd.

'I'll call if I'm passing, but I reckon you can manage between the pair of you. That was a good job you did, Todd, getting that compress on the would to staunch the blood. Hollis is in safe hands. Damn!'

Doc Halpern's bag had suddenly opened and half a dozen metal instruments clattered to the floor at Hollis's bedside. He started to bend down to retrieve them, but Todd beat him to it.

'I'll do it. An old feller that creaks in all his joints needs all the help he can get,' he said, forcing a grin.

'Don't you get uppity with me, young

man,' replied the doc in kind. 'But thanks. I must get the catch fixed on this case. Been intending to do it for weeks, but I'd have to clean it out first and I ain't never got the time. It keeps busting open.'

Todd gathered up the doc's slicing, probing, lancing instruments and carefully transferred them to the bag Halpern held open.

'One more, a scalpel. It must have skittered under the bed,' said the doc, and he started to bend down to get a look.

But Todd beat him to it again. He lay flat on his belly and saw the missing scalpel; it had fetched up against one of the bundles. He reached in, retrieved it and stood up again.

'You're right about the bag. It don't do your cutters and slicers any good being dropped on the floor. Takes the edge off them. You'll be getting a name for doing operations with a kitchen knife, Doc. Folks wouldn't stand for that. Bad for business.'

'You're right,' grinned Halpern. 'But

I ain't had any complaints so far.'

Todd started for the door but the doc didn't follow him. He wanted the doc gone, to be with his money, to put it where it would be safe. For no reason he wondered what Sarah would have said about that.

'Mustn't keep Mrs Chamberlain waiting, Doc,' he said.

'You counting on staying on here?' asked Halpern. 'I mean after Hollis is fit again?'

'No, we'll be off to have another crack at doing what we were planning.'

'What was that exactly?'

'Meantime,' said Todd, ignoring the question, 'I'd be grateful if you didn't spread the word I'm back.'

'Why not?' said Halpern in surprise.

'Truth to tell, I feel kind of foolish. You know, set out in fine style and came back with my tail between my legs. I'd rather not face folks just now. Later, maybe. We'll stay holed up here for a spell and when Hollis is able, we'll start again.'

This time, with a cheerful *adios* to Hollis, Doc Halpern moved to the door and climbed into his buggy.

'Give my regards to Mrs Chamberlain,' said Todd, 'and be sure to tell Tom from me to go easy on the whiskey bottle before he starts climbing all over barn roofs.'

Doc Halpern nodded, flicked the rump of his horse with his whip and trundled down the track that led to the main road.

Back in the cabin, Todd said: 'Think he suspects?'

'Suspects what?' said Hollis.

'About the money. Do you think he spilled his instruments on purpose so he would have an excuse to get a peek under the bed?'

'No. Nothing was said to give him ideas and you beat him to it. Like you said, he's a good man. Don't be so jittery.'

Todd wiped the sweat from his forehead with the back of his hand.

'You're right. He's a hundred per

cent human being and I'm worrying about nothing. It's the money. I ain't got used to being near so much of it.'

'Speaking of which, we'd better stash it someplace where it'll be out of sight.'

'You're right again,' said Todd and dropped to the floor, wriggled under the bed and started scooping out the bundles. As they came, he passed some to Hollis who started putting them in piles again, by denomination. When he had retrieved them all, Todd arranged the remainder. Then they counted them up so they could divide them into equal halves.

'There's one missing,' said Hollis.

'A bundle of ones,' said Todd. 'We're a hundred bucks short.'

'You must have missed one, pardner. Take another look.'

Todd bent down and looked again.

'Not here, leastways I cain't see it,' he said.

He crawled in right up to the wall.

'Nothing. But there's a crack in the floor boards wide enough for it to have fallen through. I bet that's where the varmint's gone.'

'How much?' said Hollis in a jesting voice.

'How much what?'

'You said you'd bet the bundle had dropped through the hole in the floor. How much you bet?'

'Stop paying tomfool games,' said Todd, suddenly very angry. 'This is serious.'

He backed out, got to his feet and, without dusting himself down, walked out on to the stoop. The whole cabin was propped up on stone pillars a couple of feet high to keep raccoons and other pests out. He crawled under the floor and, guided by Hollis's voice, reached the spot directly under the bed. It was dark under there. But he didn't need to look up for the crack in the floorboards: he could see the bundle lying in the dust.

'It's here,' he called. 'Just like I said. I'm coming up.'

On the stoop, he patted his clothes

and got the worst of the sand and grit out of his clothes.

He grinned as he tossed the bundle on to the pile.

'Want to count it again?' said Hollis. 'I could have hidden a couple of bundles while you were down there scrabbling in the dirt.'

Todd frowned. Hollis had said he'd chosen him for the Escobar stunt because he was the only man he could trust. Did that mean Hollis could count on him not to ask questions and do what he was told? Maybe, but the real point was this: could he trust Hollis not to leave him holding an empty bag?

'Joke,' said Hollis. 'You're letting the money get to you. I never hid no bundles. Wouldn't do such a thing. We're in this together. But I think it would be a good idea if we split it now, so we'll each have our share and there'll be no awkwardness.'

'You're right, Hollis. But with you laid up and out of it for the moment, all the responsibility's on me.'

'Sure. But you've made sure you get paid for looking after me.'

'True. But I don't reckon on making a career of playing nursemaid. You can get yourself fit again as soon as you like.'

Todd had already broken into one of the bundles of ones to pay Doc Halpern and buy supplies in Clanton. They agreed to set aside that hundred for common expenses, which left $20,000 to split. Hollis said he'd take the twenties if Todd didn't want the big denominations. Todd said that was fine by him and they ended up with Hollis getting four bundles of five dollar bills, two of tens, forty of ones and the single bundle of twenties Todd's pile was made up of four bundles of five dollar notes, two of ten dollars and sixty of ones. That made exactly $10,000 apiece: forty-seven bundles for Hollis and sixty-six for Todd.

'Hey,' said Hollis, 'your pile's bigger than mine!'

'I like mine fine,' grinned Todd. But

then the thought struck him that Hollis had outsmarted him: sixty-six bundles took more hiding and more carrying than forty-seven. There was an advantage in having the smaller number. He wasn't surprised. Hollis always was the smart one.

'What now?' he said.

They filled two saddle-bags each. Todd said he would bury his outside but couldn't do the same for Hollis, unless Hollis didn't mind him knowing where his share was hidden. Hollis said he'd keep his two in bed with him, 'to avoid misunderstandings', until he was fit enough to find a cache for them himself.

Todd went out, dug a hole at the back of a broken-down barn and covered the place with fresh dirt. Then he went inside and poured them a drink apiece. They talked about the old days and Todd started to feel better, though he couldn't quite rid himself of the feeling that Hollis had put one over on him.

A couple of days later, when Hollis was feeling stronger and sitting out on the stoop in the late afternoon sun, he said: 'When this is all over, I'm taking a train out of here. I got it planned. Train'll take me to St Louis. From there I'll go on up to New York. I got a pal there, Powys Weston, owns a shipyard, said he'll take me in as a partner if I got cash to put into the business. This far, I never had the cash. But that's stopped being a problem, so I'll take him up on it. That's what I aim to do. How about you, Todd?'

'Ain't rightly given it much thought. Losing Sarah hit me real bad. And then that norther flattening what was left of my life, when was it, jeez it was only a couple of weeks back! So I ain't had much time to adjust, let alone decide where I go next.'

'If I was you, I'd give it some thought real soon. I'm starting to feel good again so it won't be long before I take me that train to St Louis. It's never a good idea to decide what you're going to do next when you're in a fix and have to do something because then you'll do anything. You got to plan. What is it you want to do?'

'Settle down somewhere, I guess. Start over again. Get some land to work. Maybe raise a family. I don't know.'

'If I was you, I'd get away from here. You're right about Escobar. He don't give up easy and you don't want to be around when he shows up one day making enquiries about a certain sum of money he mislaid. You could go north. Since the War ended, the government's been taking land over from the Indians, some by treaty, the rest by purchase. They want pioneers to move west and settle the territory. I hear tell up north there's places where land is selling for $1.25 an acre. You could get a big spread, raise cattle, sheep. It's a good life. Or you could try your luck back east, buy yourself into a business like me.'

'I'll think about it,' said Todd.

But he couldn't put his mind to it. With time on his hands, he started thinking about the way life had gone sour on him. He couldn't stop wondering why he, who'd always worked hard, never sold anybody short, never cheated like some men he'd known, should have been treated so shabbily. How could anybody say there was justice in the world if a hardworking family man like him was handed the bucket with the hole in it?

Over the next few days, he dug up his money several times and found better places for it. Hollis got stronger and their supplies dwindled. Todd shot rabbits to eke them out but the time came when he could no longer put off riding into town.

Having no razor, neither he nor Hollis had shaved. His beard was thick enough to alter his appearance. But Jim Hicks in the stores knew him straight away.

'Ain't seen you around these parts for a while, Todd. And here you are, looking all hairy and dandy, like Abe Lincoln. You back at your place?'

Todd spun Hicks a yarn while he picked out the supplies he needed.

'Been riding round, Jim, looking for another place. The norther wrecked mine and I don't have the heart to start up there again.'

'I heard old Billy Stephens, you know, out Cottonwood Creek way, customer was telling me he's selling up. He had a stroke and is living with his daughter here in town. It's empty, ready for you to move in. Good water and grass. You could do worse.'

'Thanks, Jim, I'll be sure to go and take a looksee.'

'And I'll keep my ears open for anything else that comes up.'

Alarm bells rang in Todd's head. Damn Hicks! He'd go spraying the news that he was back all round the county.

'Be glad if you do. But don't mention my name. Folks have a way of jacking the price up if they know who's buying.

A lot of people reckon I must be made of money just because I was in the army. But it ain't so. And what I had was damned near wiped out by the norther.'

'Don't worry, I'll keep you out of it. Now that'll be $17.75 all told.'

Todd wrapped his purchases in an old sack and was hanging it on his horse's saddle when he happened to look up. Across the street, leaning against a post, smoking a cigarillo and talking to a man in Mexican clothes, was a fit looking *hombre* wearing a pair of fancy black pants and a black leather waistcoat with silver studs.

The last time Todd had seen him, his holster had been empty: it now had a big gun in it.

6

Leddy Lake

Todd swung casually, unhurriedly into the saddle, outwardly calm so as to avoid attracting attention. But his mind was racing like loco wheels.

Clanton was the town nearest to where Escobar had been jumped. It was only natural he should show up there. But if he hadn't found anything, why would he and his boys still be hanging around? What did he know? Think. He'd have asked questions. He might even have learned that a man fitting Hollis's description had been seen getting drunk in the saloon with a local man called Todd Coulter. So he might know that neither had been seen in town since just before the time he'd been jumped and robbed. But he also knew for sure that Hollis had been shot and would need a doctor. Escobar would have asked Doc Halpern, the only doc in town, if he knew anything about a yankee with a gunshot wound. But Escobar hadn't come anywhere near Ben Smiley's place. Conclusion: Doc Halpern had kept his mouth shut. And knowing he'd probably be followed was why he hadn't been back to check up on his patient. So far, so good.

But had the gaucho in the black vest recognized him?

He turned his horse into a side street, dismounted, hitched the reins to a fence post and walked back to the corner he'd just turned. He was in time to see the man the gaucho had been talking to head off at a run and the gaucho hurry cross the street and step into the stores.

That told Todd he'd been seen.

He tried to remember what he'd told Jim Hicks. As far as he could recall, he hadn't given anything away. He only hoped he was right.

Then the gaucho came out of the stores and climbed on to the horse his sidekick had fetched. He dug his heels into its ribs and raced up the street in the direction Todd was going when last seen.

Todd remounted and took a round-about route back to their hideout. He met no one on the way.

Hollis was sitting outside, gently exercising his right arm which was out of its sling. He listened grimly to what Todd had to say.

'It don't look good,' he said. 'It's only a matter of time till Escobar tracks us down, and there's only one and a half of us to fight him off. I'd do what I could, but don't count too much on me not to pass out the moment I reached for my gun. Got any ideas?'

'I figure we're safe for the moment. They hadn't got a lead on us until the gaucho . . .'

'Manolo.'

' . . . recognized me. And since I sent

him off chasing a false scent, that's the way it still is. But if they weren't sure we are still in this neck of the woods, they certainly are now. First thing: we don't panic. Second: we look for a place even more out of the way than this, where no one, not even Doc Halpern, knows we're at. So if they could go back to him and ask him again if he's seen gunshot wounds lately, and do it less politely than last time, they'd still be none the wiser.'

'You got a place in mind?'

'Think so. There's a hunting lodge up at Leddy Lake. The lake's all fished out so nobody goes there any more. I thought of it when we came here, but it was another five miles and up a stiff trail in the foothills. You wouldn't have made it. But I need to check it out. Couple of months back a family from the East passed through Clanton and there was talk of them staying a spell up there. If I go now, I'll be back by nightfall.'

'And I'll still be here. I'll rustle us up

something to eat. What did you get at the stores?'

As Todd rode out to Leddy Lake, he wondered why Hollis had gone out of his way to say he wasn't going no place. Was he planning something? Was he thinking of getting out while there was time, before Escobar caught up with them? He'd had all day to sniff around and find where Todd had hidden his share of the money. Todd wished now he'd checked it was still in the hole he'd buried it in. Hollis was getting stronger all the time. Maybe he was in better shape than he let on.

Then he told himself not to be a fool. Hollis had never done anything like that and there was no reason to think he was going to start now.

To clear his mind, he thought of Sarah. But when he did, all he could see was that expression she had when she thought he was being mean or hard or hasty. He could hear her asking what he thought he was playing at, stealing money, fooling with guns, going on the run. All the time they'd been married, he'd never strayed from the straight and narrow. And here he was, lying to Doc Halpern, hiding his face, thinking bad thoughts about Hollis Clarke who was supposed to be his best friend, for God's sake!

Leddy Lake was high in the mountains, three miles long and half a mile across. It was high enough to get cold in winter and stay cool in summer. It filled a natural basin at the bottom of a wooded valley which the Indians believed was a place of spirits before they'd been moved on to reservations. In parts, the Lake was shallow and green and there was a beach in some places; in others, the land shelved down quickly into deep, black water.

The lodge was at the deep end, where the fishing had been best. Todd reined in on the last bend before the trail started running along the lake shore. The picket fence around it was down in places, there were no animals grazing, no dogs barking, no sign of life. He rode on.

If that family from the east had stayed there, it wasn't for long. The door had no lock on it and he went in. There was dust everywhere and cobwebs hung at the windows and from the oil lamp that hung in the centre of the room. There was a potbellied stove and more furniture than Ben Smiley had left in his cabin. From both front and back, he had clear views. The area around the house had been cleared, but it was dotted with low bushes and saplings that were beginning to grow back. There was a well out back. It had everything they needed.

He sat on the front step and rolled himself a cigarette. The smoke curled up the side of his face in the still air. Sarah came into his mind again. He knew what she'd say. Give the money back. It's not yours. No good ever came of stealing. It don't buy happiness. Rich people can be just as miserable as poor people.

'But they got more money to be miserable with,' he whispered.

The sound of his voice broke the moment. He stood up, stretched, climbed back on his horse and headed back to Smiley's cabin and — if Hollis hadn't run off with all the money, he thought with a smile — supper. Tomorrow, they'd move up here.

As he approached the cabin, he saw no smoke curling up from the chimney. He rode into a stand of tall bushes and left his horse in it. His mind raced. Maybe Manolo had picked up his trail after all. If so, Todd didn't give snatch for Hollis's chances. Then it struck him that maybe Hollis had really run out on him this time, and he had to work hard to remind himself that they were supposed to be best buddies.

He watched for a while but nothing stirred. Slowly he crept out from the greenery that hid him and started towards the cabin, making the most of the cover. He had got about half way, with about fifty yards to go, when

Hollis appeared on the stoop and waved.

'Come on in. The excitement's all over.'

Todd stood up, holstered his gun, whistled for his horse and joined Hollis.

'What excitement?' he said.

'About an hour after you'd gone, I went in the house. I thought I'd do something useful, clean my gun. There was blood in the chamber. It wasn't jammed, but it wasn't moving free. So I scraped it clean and oiled it and loaded up. I'd just finished when I heard a sound. I turned and there in the doorway was a guy I never saw before. He was looking straight at me. He made a move with his right hand. I drew before he could and got my shot in. The range was so close I couldn't miss.'

'Was it Manolo?'

'Nope.'

'Or another of Escobar's boys?'

'I never saw him before.'

'Where's he now?'

'I dragged him over to the barn with the roof.'

'Is he dead?'

'As a brick.'

'See anybody else?'

'It was all quiet until you showed up, though I only spotted you because I was looking out for you. I thought the guy could have had a friend who'd stayed out there.'

Todd crossed to the barn, with Hollis in tow.

On the bare earth was the body of a man Todd didn't want to see.

'You damn fool!' he snarled. 'That's not one of Escobar's men. It's Mick Murphy! You shot him, you crazy loon!'

'Your neighbour? Jeez, I'm sorry, Todd. But he snuck up and he made that movement with his hand. I could have sworn he was going for his gun. I reacted. You'd have done the same if a guy you never saw before had come up on you like that.'

Hollis was probably right. And that was the terrible thing. Not a month ago, nothing had been too much trouble for Mick and Annie. They'd probably saved his life with their kindness. And now Mick was dead. Killed not by a badman but by the money. And, like Hollis said, if it had been the other way round and he'd been cleaning his gun, more than likely he'd have been the one who'd killed Mick. His anger died in his throat and he heard himself say:

'Come on, let's get supper. We'll bury him in the morning.'

'Not so fast, Todd, you ain't thinking straight. I'm assuming your friend wasn't out riding and just stopped by, on the off-chance, for a glass of water: he must have come because he knew you were here. Ask yourself this: how did he know where to find you? And if he knew, how long before Escobar gets to find out too? We got to get out now, tonight. I got our stuff together, the blankets and supplies you got from the stores. Go dig up your money and we're out of here.'

Hollis was right.

It took them just ten minutes to load the horses, but longer to bury Mick in the woods. No way could they leave the body in the barn to tell a tale that might lead back to them. Hollis found Mick's horse which they led for part of the way up to Leddy Lake and then released to find its own way home. It would look like Mick had been thrown or otherwise come to grief and a party would go out searching for him. But his death would stay a mystery.

In his ear, Sarah said: 'How could you do such a terrible thing to Annie? I'm ashamed of you. You've got to stop this madness now before it causes any more misery!'

'How much further, Todd?'

Hollis was suffering. The higher they went the colder it got. Todd took a strange comfort from this confirmation that his partner was a long way off fitness. It made him feel more in charge.

By the time they got to the lodge it

was dark. But there was a moon and by its light they skirted the lake's edge and entered the lodge. Hollis collapsed into a chair. Todd busied around, lit the stove with cut logs from the store and made something to eat.

Afterwards, they finished the rest of the coffee and smoked.

'This ain't working out as planned, old friend,' said Hollis. 'By rights, I should be in New York drinking whiskey with Powys Weston, celebrating me being his new partner. But here I am, sitting in a shack, hurting and feeling like it's going to be a long time before I get on that train.'

'You're just tired, Hollis. You'll see things different in the morning.'

Hollis felt just the same when the sun came up. But over the next few days, he grew stronger and his mood lightened. Maybe it was being by the lake and on a mountain where the air was more bracing than down on the hot and dusty plain. Whatever the reason, he got to move his arm more freely each day and he stopped feeling whacked if he got out of his chair. One day when Todd had gone out looking for something to shoot for supper, he even managed to go fifty yards from the lodge and dig a hole for his money.

That was the first thing Todd had done after Hollis had settled down on that first night. He had moved his money several times since.

They had been there a week when Pete Meacher turned up out of the blue.

Pete was a roughneck, an odd-jobbing man who lived a wastrel life. He was light-fingered and when he had enough money which he'd come by honestly or dishonestly, he got drunk in one of Clanton's watering holes. He gambled too. In Todd's book, Pete was as trustworthy as a rattler, only he didn't rattle to let you know when he would strike. He didn't know this for sure. It was just a feeling. A lot of men liked Pete, bought him drinks, thought he was good company.

'I never knew there was anybody in

the old lodge,' Pete said, 'let alone you, Todd, though I ain't seen you around for a spell. How you been? I was sorry to hear you lost your place in that norther. Northers are bitches.'

Todd was alone. Hollis had gone for a walk, to stretch his leg muscles.

'You here all alone?'

'Sure am,' said Todd. 'Only place I could think of. There was nothing left of the house after the storm. What brings you up here? I ain't seen a soul in weeks.'

'Looking for Mick Murphy.'

'Something happened to him?'

'Maybe. He rode out about a week ago and hasn't been seen since. His horse came back but not him.'

'I sure am sorry to hear it. He was a good man.'

'You say 'was' like he's dead. He's only missing.'

'Of course. Sorry. I just assumed . . . it's been a week . . . the chance of him being alive . . . '

'Anyway, some of the fellers been

doing the rounds, keeping an eye out for him. So you never saw hide nor hair of him?'

'Like I said, I ain't seen anybody for weeks.'

'Well, when you do, tell him to come home. Annie's in a state.'

'I sure will.'

When Pete had gone, Hollis came out of the woods.

'Who was that?'

'Pete Meacher. Part-time drunk.'

'What did he want?'

'Looking for Mick.'

'Maybe,' said Hollis. 'You sure that's all there was to his visit? What are the chances of him being on Escobar's payroll? Looking for Mick is a pretty good excuse for looking for other things.'

'I never had much time for him, but one thing I know for sure: reliable he ain't. I can't see Escobar putting much faith in anything he said. He'd make up a story for a dollar to get drunk on.'

'So we give him the benefit of the doubt?'

'I guess so.'

But he was not as confident as he sounded. When he went out he kept his eyes peeled and he looked regularly over his shoulder. That night, he slept more lightly than usual.

Next morning, over the same flapjacks they'd been eating for a week, Todd said: 'I been a rich man for more than a month. But I haven't spent a cent on what rich men spend their money on. I ain't even seen a steak or had me a decent shave in a barber's parlour. Where I've been, except for a couple of trips into Clanton to buy supplies, there ain't no call for money 'cos there's no streets, no stores, and nothing to buy. All the money's good for out here is for burning on a fire to keep warm by.'

'You got to have patience,' said Hollis calmly.

Suddenly Todd could no longer bear to hear that calm, reasonable voice. He stood up so quickly he knocked his chair over.

'What I want to know is how much

longer is this going on? When will you be fit enough to look after yourself? I'm tired of holding your hand.'

'And I'm tired of having you hold it,' said Hollis. 'Though as I recall, you're being paid handsome for doing it.'

'I don't need your money,' snarled Todd. 'I just want to get away. I want to be somewhere else and not living this hole-in-a-corner life with a cripple who's cramping my style.'

Hollis did not reply but looked at him thoughtfully.

'Know what, Todd? I reckon we've come to the end of the road, you and me. It had to happen sooner or later. If I hadn't taken that bullet, we'd have split and gone our separate ways long since, as planned, good friends and not a cross word between us. But we had to stay together. You saved my life and I'll always be thankful for that. But it's no good if we start growling at each other, showing our teeth, not with all that money sitting out there, waiting to be dug up and taken. It's too much temptation in a small place. We been too close together for too long. One of these days, you or I will say a word out of place. One of us will get suspicious. One thing will lead to another and the lead will fly. I don't want that. I'm well on the mend but I still got to build up my strength. So, seeing as how you're the fittest, I think you should take your stuff and go.'

Todd thought: why should I be the one to have to go? Hollis always makes sure he gets the best deal. Always did. I don't know why I've stuck with him. But the hell with it. It's the last time. Anything to get away from that self-satisfied —

'On the other hand,' said Hollis, breaking into his thoughts, 'I think we've left it a tatch late.'

Todd turned and looked out through the window and saw what Hollis had seen.

'Escobar!' he breathed.

7

The Big Knuckle

At the edge of the woods, half a mile away, just where the trail hit the lakeshore and turned along it towards the lodge, half a dozen riders had halted. They had the sun in their eyes. It was still early and its rays were almost horizontal. The lead rider cupped both hands for eyeshades and stared at the lodge. Then he turned and said something to the man nearest him who was Manolo.

'They know we're here,' said Todd. 'They've seen the smoke.'

'I make out Escobar, Manolo . . . '

'And Pete Meacher. The others I can't tell about from here. But Escobar won't have had any trouble recruiting extra guns.'

'We can't let them pin us down here. We're outnumbered and we ain't got much ammo . . . '

'And no one to bring us more,' said Todd with a grin.

'Save the jokes, we got nothing to laugh about. They could just sit down, smoke those damned cheroots they like so much and wait until we have to come out with our hands up and without a shot fired. We can't stay here, right? We go now, and we got a chance. You saddle up and I'll get some stores together.'

'What about the money?'

'We both hid our shares,' said Hollis. 'I hid mine pretty good so no animals of either the two-legged or four-legged sort could dig it up again. I guess you did the same with yours. So let it stay where it is. We come back for it later.'

'And what if we don't?'

'Then Escobar won't get it either. Agreed?'

'Agreed.'

While Hollis scooped up dry food

goods and a few basic utensils and filled a couple of sacks with them, Todd slipped quietly out the back way. Keeping a wary eye open, he reached the stables, saddled the horses and brought them to the back door. Hollis was waiting for him. They slung the sacks over their pommels and started walking their mounts through the woods because it was quieter than riding them, taking care to keep the lodge between them and Escobar's men. They'd made fifty yards when they heard a voice shout:

'Hey, gringos! You in yor 'ouse? I yor fren'. You commin' out? We 'ave leetle talk?'

'Escobar's been working on his English,' said Hollis. 'But he don't say anything more worth hearing in English than in Spanish.'

'You commin' out?'

The voice was fainter now.

'How well do you know this neck of the woods?' asked Hollis.

'Pretty well. At the start, before we

had Phil, Sarah and me used to come up and spend time here. One time, I rode clear round the lake. Another day I climbed the hill over the water from the lodge. We used to call it the Big Knuckle on account of it looking like one. Never found out if it has another name. Got me a grand view from up there.'

'What's on the other side of your Big Knuckle?'

'More of the same,' said Todd. 'Hills and dales and rivers and trees. Lots of trees. No one ever crossed it as far as I know. It's a wilderness, mighty hard going.'

'You know a place up there where we can hide away until Escobar gets so tired of chasing us that he'll give up?'

The sound of Escobar's voice floated through the woods. The words were indistinct, but the shots that followed made up for them; they were very clear.

'They're getting impatient,' said Hollis.

'How fit you reckon you are?' asked Todd.

'Don't worry none about me. I'll keep up.'

'In that case, we ride round the bottom of the lake and get some height on the Knuckle. There was a gold-rush up there fifteen, twenty years ago. It petered out. But there are places up there full of workings, old levels and mines. There's enough holes in the ground up there to hide an army.'

'Sounds good,' said Hollis. 'And there's a big back door. If ever we get cornered, we just take off over the other side of the mountain. Let's go.'

Now that there was no danger of being heard, they mounted their horses and moved more quickly through the sparse undergrowth. From time to time they heard more shots. Then there was silence.

'I guess they found out we're not home,' said Hollis. 'They'll be coming after us, so let's get going.'

They quickened the pace. Even so, whenever they came to a stream, they took time out to separate, one going left and the other right, wading the stream for a hundred paces and then joining up further along, covering their tracks and hiding all trace of their passage to slow their followers down.

They skirted the bottom end of the lake, dismounting to lead their horses over the outflow, then started gaining height. Behind them, the lake dropped away.

'Not much further,' said Todd. 'I remember that rock formation there.' And he pointed to a split boulder with a sapling growing out of the middle of it.

They skirted the rock and saw that the ground levelled out and made a wide shelf against a wall honeycombed with holes. There were piles of spoil and boulders which had fallen from the cliff above. Below was a slope of scree which dropped away steeply.

'Take your pick,' Todd grinned.

He was feeling better than he had for weeks, since before the norther had hammered the last nail into his life. The doubts and suspicions had vanished; it was like a weight taken off his shoulders. Action! A common foe! It was like being back in the army where you knew your enemy and all you had to do was point a gun at him when the time was right and shoot. Maybe he'd relaxed because he was doing something with a purpose to it. Then he realized he hadn't thought about the money all day. Maybe it was the money that had been making him twitchy.

They hadn't reached the shelf any too soon for Hollis. He had started to tire badly, but he was far from spent. While Todd tethered the horses in the largest of the shafts and tunnels, he looked the rest over and chose one at the edge of the shelf which commanded a clear view of the trail they'd come up by. If they set up camp there, they'd have plenty of warning if Escobar managed to track them this far. Then he saw that to the right of the tunnel entrance was a curtain of rock which hid a cleft, or funnel, which could be climbed. If they were cornered, they'd have a way out. It was the perfect place.

He began piling rocks at the entrance to form a protective barricade they could defend from. Todd returned with the saddle-bags and a water canteen which he'd filled from a stream at the far end of the natural terrace and helped him build the parapet. Then they drank some water, ate dry biscuit and, while the sun sank behind the jagged horizon, looked down on the route they'd climbed. Nothing moved.

Then a squirrel came from nowhere, scuttered among the loose stones in front of the tunnel mouth and stopped when it found a nut. As it ate with quick-chomping jaws, it stared at the two men, inquisitively, without fear. Then, in its own time, it scampered off unconcernedly, leaving the nut half eaten.

When it was dark, Todd cooked up a meal. The smoke didn't show against the night sky.

They woke with the dawn. The early coolness soon receded and it was another warm, still day. They resumed their vigil. Sooner or later Escobar would have to give up. All they had to do was to sit tight and wait for him to abandon the chase. Time passed. It looked like Escobar had lost the scent. Then they heard voices.

Todd took out his gun. Hollis crawled to the lip of the ledge and risked a peek over. Below them Escobar was leading his men up a slope on a course that would take them fifty yards to the right of the mine workings. They looked weary and their horses clearly didn't like the steep pitch of the slope. Hollis watched for a while and turned to motion to Todd to come and get a closer look. As he did so, he dislodged a medium sized rock which rolled down the scree slope gathering speed as it went, starting small avalanches of stones which rattled down the mountain before stopping in a deafening silence.

''Oo made det noise?' said Escobar.

'Be just an animal, a jackrabbit, a raccoon, how should I know,' said Pete Meacher.

Hollis and Todd froze.

'Go to look,' said Escobar. 'You an' 'eem,' he added, waving at the nearest man.

Todd now saw there were seven of them, not six. In addition to the two Spaniards and Pete Meacher, he recognized Charlie Denner, a hand for hire like Pete, and Abel Laufman, who had once rustled three of his steers, though nothing could be proved. The remaining two looked like professional guns. It was a strong line-up. One of the guns had been designated by Escobar to keep Meacher company.

Meacher went first, and then the gun started climbing up the loose scree, two steps forward and one step back up the unstable, shifting stones. When they were half way up, Hollis lobbed a stone away to his right. The idea was to distract attention, confirm what Meacher said about the noise being caused by an animal. It landed with a clatter and another small avalanche began. Immediately the professional gun, who had climbed faster than Meacher, had a Colt in his hand and was shooting at the noise.

When the echoes had died away, he called out: '*Es nada*, 'ees notting 'ere.'

As he turned to make his way back to where Escobar watched from his horse, he seemed to stumble, his feet shot from under him and he sat down hard. Immediately, the whole slope rippled, shuddered and started moving. He disappeared under tons of scree and shale which then ran down Meacher in an unstoppable wave and carried both men over a steep drop and into the woods below. When the dust settled, the slope was bare.

Escobar looked furious at losing two men.

'Well I'll be damned,' said Todd in a whisper.

'Two down, five to go,' Hollis whispered back.

Just then, one of their horses stabled in the level further along the terrace snickered.

Escobar's head came up. 'Sombody

up der!' he shouted and he stared at the ledge above him, looking for a way up.

'*Arriba!*' he said and made his meaning clear by urging his horse up into the trees bordering the bare slope from which the scree had been scraped like mud off a boot. His men followed him.

It was the signal for Todd and Hollis to blaze away in the hope of reducing the odds still further. The remaining gunslinger was hit and fell off his horse which rolled on him then got up and raced away wild-eyed into the safety of the woods. Todd thought he'd winged Denner but wasn't sure. His other shots spanged off rocks and ended harmlessly embedded in tree trunks.

Then suddenly the space below was empty and all that could be heard was the sound of retreating horses. The prone gunman didn't move, didn't get up.

'What's Escobar's next move?' asked Todd as he reloaded.

'In his place, I'd organize a diversion

and a pincer movement. Come on, let's get back to the tunnel. We're exposed here, sitting targets.'

They settled down behind the barricade to wait. Maybe twenty minutes passed. Then Todd said: 'Here comes your diversion.'

Stripped of scree, the slope below the shelf which had been so unsafe, was now an easy climb. It must have been, for a hat had appeared over the lip. Todd shot it off. But it was not the start of a frontal attack but a fishing expedition, for the hat hadn't been on a head but on a stick. A second hat appeared to the left. Todd shot that off too. Another stick. But a movement out of a corner of one eye showed the man — it was Laufman — who'd waved the first hat heaving himself up on to level ground. He skipped quickly out of sight behind one of the boulders littering the shelf. From there he loosed off shots which were wild but dangerous enough to make the defenders keep their heads down. This gave Denner, the second man, a chance to follow Laufman on to level ground. So Todd hadn't winged Denner after all. At close intervals, they shot at the barricade, less in hope of hitting the men in the tunnel than of pinning them down.

'I don't like this,' said Todd. 'Denner and Laufman have got us pinned down with Escobar and Manolo out there on the loose where we can't see them.'

He poked his Colt over the barricade and fired at Denner's rock.

'I don't know what they got in mind,' said Hollis, 'but they sure won't aim to kill us. At least not straight off. Escobar don't know if we've got the money with us. If we've hidden it and we get shot, he'll never get his hands on it. He has to take us alive.'

'Hey, gringos!' came a voice from their left. 'You wanna deal? I say you com out. You give me ma money. You go hom. Is deal?'

Todd heard a scuffling noise to his right and turned just in time to see an arm in a black shirtsleeve appear round the tunnel mouth. At the end of the arm was a hand. The hand had a gun in it. The gun fired blindly. The shot hit a wall and screamed harmlessly into the darkness. Todd shot back but the arm disappeared too fast. It was Manolo.

'Maybe you're right about him wanting to take us alive, but one of us would serve his purpose,' said Todd. 'I think this has got personal with him. Escobar doesn't like you at all. You bested him and he won't stand for it. Poor loser. He wants to even the score just as much as he wants the money.'

'You may be right or you may be wrong. But we won't argue the point. It's time to get out of here.'

Crawling on their bellies, Hollis first, they slid behind the rock curtain and started to climb.

'Excuse!' came Escobar's voice. 'Was mistake. Manolo don' lissen. Bad boy, Manolo!'

Loose stones clattered down the funnel as they gained height. Denner was first to realize what was going on.

He stood up and started running towards the tunnel shouting: 'They're getting away!' though he couldn't figure out how. Only when he reached the mouth of the tunnel did he see the curtain of rock which hid the fault in the cliff face. He squeezed into it and looked up. As he did so, a single bullet from Todd's gun entered his left eye. His last act was to fall against Laufman who had followed hard on his heels. By the time Escobar cottoned on to what was happening, Hollis first and then Todd had reached the top and had flopped, gasping for breath, on a flat rock in the sun.

The funnel channelled the sound of Escobar's voice which they heard yelling at Laufman, ordering him to pull Denner's body clear and climb up after the Yankees. But they also heard Laufman say no. Twice. Then there was a shot and they didn't hear Laufman say anything else.

'Come on,' said Todd. 'At this point we get out of here.'

'Over the Knuckle and down the other side?'

'Nope. We got no horses or supplies and that's real wild country there. Even if we get away from Escobar, I wouldn't give two beans for our chances of getting out alive. No, we go back and face them. End it now. We're doing fine so far. They was seven. Now there's just the two of them.'

'You're right,' said Hollis. 'There's also the money to consider. The further we go travelling over hill and dale the further we get from the money. Escobar might follow us for a while, give up and go back to the lodge, start searching and dig it up. He might get lucky: he's got two chances.'

Todd was brought up short. How come he kept forgetting the money? But Hollis was right. This was all about the money. It made no sense to put a lot of distance between them and what they'd fought for. He wanted a showdown, face to face with Escobar. He wanted him off his back for good. But it wasn't an end in itself. It meant getting rid of an obstacle between him and his money.

They needed to find a way back down, a route that would bring them out at Escobar's rear. The funnel they'd climbed up was too dangerous. They scouted in both directions, looking for a gully or another cleft in the rock that would take them back down to the level shelf. Todd spotted a faint animal track which looked promising. They followed it down and they came out about thirty yards from the level where they'd stabled their horses. There was no sign of Escobar or Manolo.

Carefully, with guns drawn, they crept along the face of the cliff, keeping as close to it as they could and stepping into abandoned shafts and recesses in the rock wall for cover. And still there was no Escobar.

They were about ten yards from the mouth of the tunnel they'd used as a base when he walked out of it, with Manolo a step behind. If Escobar was surprised, he didn't show it.

'Ah, Yankee!' he said, with a smile that displayed all those teeth. 'You com see Escobar, yes? You tell Escobar where is money! *El dinero no es a lí, es a mí!* 'Ees my money!'

Todd moved a yard to Hollis's right to give himself room. His gun was still in his hand and he kept it pointed at Escobar who stood his ground, waiting for an answer, his smile as broad as ever. Manolo also moved away from his boss's left, which left the four men facing each other forming a small square.

'*Quizás*,' said Hollis, 'maybe. I stole it from you, you stole it from God knows who, and they probably stole it from a long line of thieves. Possession being most of the law, that dinero belongs to whoever's got it. At the moment, we're the ones looking after it. You want it, you take it.'

Escobar stopped smiling and spread his arms wide, a gesture almost of surrender. It took the Yankees off guard.

Manolo used that split second to draw his gun. But he didn't get a shot off. Todd hardly aimed but his bullet found its target. The Mexican staggered under the impact, looked up in surprise and fell backwards on to the ground. Escobar jumped forward and grabbed Hollis who, still far from peak fitness, was slow to react. He turned and faced Todd using Hollis as a human shield.

'You, gringo!' he snarled, with no hint of a smile now, and without a second glance at Manolo lying lifeless in the dust, 'you say where is money or say *adios* to yor fren.'

He had a large hunting knife pressed so hard against Hollis's neck that the skin broke. A small trickle of blood ran down.

Todd hesitated. He didn't feel he was good enough with a gun to take Escobar. Escobar was a small target; there was a good chance he would miss him altogether, and a better chance that he'd hit Hollis instead.

And then he realized he was holding

a gun at two men who stood between him and *all the money*. He wouldn't shed tears for Escobar. But with Hollis gone, and no questions asked — no one ever came this high on the Knuckle any more, the bodies would never be found — he'd have the full $20,000. And he wouldn't have to worry any more about having Escobar on his tail or Hollis muscling in on him.

Sarah said: 'What are you thinking of? Hollis is your friend! What mess have you got yourself into? You're an honest man, decent and hard-working. But you've let all this money go to your head. Now put those nasty thoughts out of your mind and *shoot the damn Mex*!'

He was thinking he'd never remembered Sarah talking like that as he tightened his finger on the trigger of his raised Colt and mechanically, with only part of his mind, fired.

A small red spot appeared in Escobar's forehead and his eyes went out, like a candle in a strong wind. His grip on the knife slackened and it fell to the ground. Then he sagged, his legs buckled and he went down, his weight dragging Hollis with him.

'You took some chance there, pardner,' Hollis said, getting to his feet and dusting himself down. 'I didn't know you could shoot that straight.'

'Sarah would have been proud of me,' said Todd with a grin.

Hollis looked at his friend.

'Sure she would,' he said and meant it. Still he thought it was a strange thing to say all the same.

8

Wood Shavings

They buried the bodies.

In his ear he heard Sarah say: 'I don't know about Denner and Laufman, but I think the world's more peaceful without Escobar and Manolo in it.'

Todd, who had shot three of the five corpses, took some comfort from that.

He was all for packing up and heading off back to the lodge. There was enough sky between the sun and the western horizon for them to make it back before dark. But Hollis wanted to know what was the hurry. They'd had a big day and he'd move all the faster after a night to get over it.

Todd was getting tired of hanging around waiting for his old buddy to recover. He'd been looking after him, waiting for him to get over it for weeks. It was what they'd agreed; he was being paid to do it, but Hollis sure was taking his time to get fit again. But he said nothing, shot a jackrabbit and cooked up supper.

Next day they went down the mountain, crossed the outflow and rode back slowly through the woods to the lodge.

The door hung off its hinges, the windows had been shot out and the place had been ransacked. Escobar would probably have burned it down if he hadn't been so anxious to get after them. But before going inside Todd walked into the woods by himself, to check that nobody had been near the place where he'd stashed his money. It was undisturbed in its patch of poison ivy under a tall pine, a hundred yards from the lodge. He didn't go near it, just in case someone happened to see him — 'you mean Hollis', Sarah whispered in his ear — and checked it from a distance. It was a weight off his mind.

Todd fixed the door and tidied the place up.

While they ate supper, Hollis started reminiscing about the old days. But Todd wasn't interested. He wanted to know what plans Hollis had, how much longer he thought it would be before they split up and went their separate ways, just like they'd planned.

'Hold on, pardner,' he said, holding up one hand. 'Slow down. I reckon I'm just about there. Give it a week, ten days, and I'll be back to normal.'

Todd started counting the days off. After a week, Hollis said he was as near to his old self as he needed to be. To prove it, he went outside and starting splitting logs. Todd stayed indoors getting supper, filling his mind with the thought that he was richer than anybody he'd ever known and yet he spent all his time running around after a sick man and doing chores like he was a servant or poor relation. Then he was suddenly aware that he couldn't hear the thwack of the axe any more. He looked up and saw Hollis leaning against the door jamb, his right arm hanging loose, with blood dripping from the fingers.

'I guess I wasn't as ready as I thought. The wound's opened up.'

Todd nearly chewed his knuckles with frustration. Another day or so and he would have been free. If Hollis had waited a mite longer, he could have tried swinging from the trees or crushing rocks with his bare hands or taking all the tomfool risks he wanted for all Todd cared. But now the chump-head had spoiled everything.

He sat Hollis down and peeled off his shirt. The scar had more or less healed but the new pink skin wasn't tough enough for swinging axes. The lips had opened and the blood oozed out. Todd bound it up (he was getting good at it because he'd had so much damn practice, he told himself bitterly) and hung the arm in a sling. Then he told Hollis to sit down and not move.

Then he went on with the supper,

thinking that this would set Hollis's recovery back weeks.

Though it turned out the wound was superficial, not deep, and started to mend quickly, Todd couldn't throw off his frustration. It was so bad he preferred to be by himself and got away from Hollis as soon as he could each day. He spent more and more time out of the house; he said he wanted to explore the lake and the woods and hills around it. Setting off soon after sunup, he wouldn't get back sometimes until it was getting dark. The exercise tired him and took his mind off the way Hollis had trapped him.

One day, he got back a little earlier. Hollis wasn't on the porch like he usually was nor indoors or in the stables. Todd was suddenly suspicious, went out to the place where his money was buried. He was astounded to see Hollis standing by the pine, looking down at the patch of poison ivy.

It was obvious what he was up to.

The next day, he came back at the

same time. Again Hollis wasn't home. But he was nowhere near the pine either, though that didn't mean a thing. It was more than likely he'd spotted Todd the previous day and was deliberately avoiding the place where the money was. That night, Todd went out, dug it up by moonlight and reburied it in a shallow depression, near a small rock that put him in mind of a buffalo's head.

'I guess you noticed that patch of poison ivy?' said Hollis that night.

'Sure I seen it. What about it?'

'Just pointing it out in case you hadn't. You don't want to go walking through that. I rolled in some when I was a kid. Took months before it faded.'

'That the only reason you asked?'

'What other reason would I have?' said Hollis in surprise.

'I moved it.'

'Moved what?'

'Don't give me that,' snapped Todd, who could feel his self-control going. 'I saw you day before yesterday, hanging around where I had my stash.'

'You think I want to *steal* your stash?' said Hollis incredulously.

'You don't expect me to believe it was just coincidence that I saw you looking at the very place where I hid it?'

'Listen to me, Todd. I saw poison ivy, that's all. I wasn't thinking about money, mine or yours. I'm not interested in your money. I got my own. So let it go.'

Not trusting himself to speak, Todd went outside and walked down to the lake. It was a while before he felt calm again.

Although it was now out in the open, the tension between them remained high. They hardly spoke to each other for two days. Then Hollis broke the silence.

'What's got into you, Todd? Cat's got your tongue for sure.'

'Got nothing to say,' said Todd.

'Look, I'm sorry. It's my fault you're cooped up here. But I can manage now. I'm grateful for everything you've done but I'll be fine. There's no need for you to stay.'

'Maybe you're right. I got the itch to move on.'

'There's more to it than that. I don't know what's got into you. You take your gun to bed with you at night as if you expect the place is going to be raided. You should be feeling light as air. You don't act like you're rich.'

'Why don't you shut your trap, Hollis? I'll pack my things and be out of your hair first thing tomorrow.'

'I don't like that look you get in your eye, Todd. It's the same one I saw the day you shot Escobar, when you were pointing the Colt. I couldn't tell if you wanted to shoot me more than him.'

'Well maybe it would help if you stopped snooping around where I hide my share of the money.'

'You still think I want your money? Well I don't. Ten grand is more than enough for what I need. Why would I want yours?'

Todd looked away. Why did men

want money? Because however much they had, it was never enough. Every one knew that.

'I'm turning in,' he said.

In the morning he was up early. He saddled his horse, dug up his money from the shallow depression near the rock that reminded him of a buffalo's head, and left without even saying goodbye. He felt relieved. The way things were going, he and Hollis would soon have been shooting at each other.

He'd filled many sleepless nights dreaming about what he'd do once he was free of Hollis. He'd head back to Clanton and probably stay a while, put up at the hotel, have a good time, buy some dude clothes, drink some whiskey, spend some of those bills. Then he'd buy a rail ticket and take off in the direction of . . . That was as far as he usually got, not because he fell asleep but because he couldn't make up his mind what to do next. With all that money, the world was his oyster. But which way was best? East or west?

Maybe north. Or perhaps south was better?

Then there was the problem of looking after the money. Maybe it wouldn't be such a good idea to put up in the hotel and start spending. People would be curious and ask questions about how he got rich and spin hard-up stories so he'd give them some of what had been so hard come by. And where would he keep his money? He didn't trust banks, banks got robbed. But he couldn't leave it in a bag in his room where anyone could come in off the street and walk off with it. Bury it again? Where? If Hollis could smell out his stash in the poison ivy, there'd be others just as able to find it in a hole in a rock or in the back of a cave. Even as he thought this thought, he had the strange feeling that he was being watched. But though he kept a keen eye out from then on, he saw no one.

Since he had to go somewhere, he thought he'd hole up for a while at Cottonwood Creek, the place Jim Hicks had told him about. He couldn't go back to Ben Smiley's, not with Mick Murphy buried there: too many ghosts. He'd get more peace on Billy Stephens' place, have time to sort himself out and decide where to go.

He reached the Creek not long after noon. The cabin looked just like Billy Stephens had just stepped out and would be back any moment. The door wasn't locked and Todd moved straight in. The furniture was all there but the cupboards were empty. He'd have to go into town and get provisioned up. For how long? Not more than a week, maybe two, he swore.

But the first job was to find a safe place for the money. He'd need cash to buy supplies. He opened the bag and laid his share out on the table: sixty bundles of singles, four of five dollar bills and two of ten. Sixty-six in all.

He arranged them in different ways. Singles in a cube, then the fives and last the tens on the top. Next he made a square, a circle, a triangle of the ones and arranged the fives and tens in patterns inside them then outside them. He sat back and stared at them. Whatever shape he put them in, they always totted up to $10,000. Ten thousand! Todd felt dizzy at the thought of it. He riffled through the bundles. They made a whirring noise but they also gave off a smell of damp. That was because they'd been buried in the shady woods up at Leddy Lake. He didn't like that smell much. A smell of decay. Next time he'd find somewhere drier.

He broke into one bundle of tens and also took out twenty or so singles and pushed them into his back pocket. He put all sixty-six bundles back in the bag and pushed it under a couch, where it couldn't be seen. Outside, just beyond the wood store was a small, windowless lean-to which had a stack of tools in it. He selected a pick and shovel and walked for about fifty yards behind the house until he found what he was looking for, a clump of bushes growing low next to a picket fence.

He ducked under the bush, held the low branches back with one hand and with the other jabbed at the soft earth until he'd made a hole two feet square and two deep. He returned to the house, retrieved the bag, laid it in the hole and with the shovel covered the bag with the soil until the hole was filled. He lobbed a few stones casually around it and left the place looking as natural and undisturbed as at any time since the days of Adam and Eve. Then he saddled up and rode into town.

Jim Hicks was surprised to see him.

'Thought you must have packed up and gone for good,' he said. 'I always had you down as the settled sort that stayed on the farm. Not one to stray. But you disappear for weeks and then pop up like a jack-in-the-box. What can I get you?'

While Hicks bustled round getting coffee, flour, beans, beef jerky and the rest of it, Todd spun him the yarn he'd prepared. How his friend Hollis Clarke hadn't been getting over his gunshot wound over at Ben Smiley's and how they'd reckoned a spell up at Leddy Lake, where it was cooler, would help him mend faster. How it had worked and how Hollis had taken off.

'Glad to hear the patient's fully recovered,' said the voice of Doc Halpern. 'I thought I recognized the horse outside. Came in to say hello.'

'Hi, Doc. Yep, Hollis is as fit as a flea. He's gone.'

'I thought the pair of you was going to try your luck together out west?'

'Change of plan. I guess Hollis has got more adventure in him than me. We called it off, or rather I backed down. I like staying where I'm at.'

'I was just saying the same thing,' said Hicks and then, in the same breath: 'Twelve dollars fifty.'

'He's still missing,' said Doc Halpern.

Todd looked blank.

'Mick. Mick Murphy.'

'Oh yes, Mick. Sorry, my mind was on Hollis. Been too long together, just the two of us. End up with a narrow outlook on things.'

'And a short memory,' said the doc. Todd heard the disapproval in his voice. 'No sign of him. Can't make it out. The sheriff's organized a few searches. Nothing. He could be anywhere.'

'I'll keep my eyes peeled. I'll let you know if I come up with anything. I'm out at Billy Stephen's place. Where'd you say his daughter lives, Jim? I ought to check with him if it's OK to stay there for a spell. Be polite.'

'She lives opposite the church but he won't mind,' said Hicks. 'Be glad to have someone in the place. Look after it. Keep the wildlife out.'

'You could say hello to Annie at the same time.'

'Annie?'

'You sure you haven't taken a hit to the head, Todd?' said the doc. 'Annie Murphy. She's taking it bad, not knowing if Mick's dead or alive. Billy's daughter had a room spare, she rattles around like a pea in that big old house, so she said for her to come in to town. That way she'd have company instead of being stuck out on the farm on her own. It would be kind if you said a few words. I heard she and Mick were good to you after you lost Sarah.'

The reproach in the doc's voice was not lost on Todd. He kicked himself. How could he forget about Annie and act so much out of character at a time when the last thing he needed was to draw attention to himself? He liked Annie a lot. He wouldn't do anything to hurt her. He wasn't that sort of man.

'I didn't know she was in town. I was going to ride out and see how she was doing. Glad you told me, Doc.'

Doc Halpern nodded, but Todd could see he wasn't convinced.

Molly Stephens said it was fine for Todd to stay out at Cottonwood Creek.

'Sorry to hear about Mick,' said Todd. 'He was a good man.'

'Was?' said Annie. 'Unless you know something that says he's dead, I'd prefer it if you didn't talk as if he was.'

Todd didn't stay long but took his leave and made for the saloon. He needed a drink.

It was early and quiet. He drank down the whiskey at the bar and ordered another. While it was coming, he looked up into the back bar mirror and surveyed the room behind him. A few cowhands with no work on and a few strangers were sitting around idling. Among the strangers were the usual passengers waiting for the stage: a portly gent in a brown derby who he put down as a commercial traveller, a reverend in a high collar and a couple of men in fancy Mexican-style clothes. They'd all looked up as he came in and had then lost interest. Just another quiet day in Clanton.

Back at Cottonwood Creek, he sat on the stoop smoking and drinking from the pint of rye he'd bought.

Clanton folk hadn't given him an easy ride but he'd come through it. Jim Hicks had swallowed his story and if Doc Halpern had seemed a mite suspicious, he had nothing to go on. Not remembering about Mick had made him look bad. But he'd talked his way out of it. Even Annie had perked up by the time he left.

After a while, he looked around and found Billy's fishing rod. He went a little way up the creek, sat on the bank and let his line drift in the slow current.

He tried to fix his mind on what he was going to do now that he could do anything, have anything, go anywhere. He knew he deserved the money; he felt it was his revenge on the world for Sarah and Phil and the norther. It was his due, his payback. Wasn't he known for being a good sort of man? Isn't that what Hicks had said? Wasn't that what the doc thought? Still, he couldn't forget the killing he'd done. Denner and Manolo he put down to self-defence. But he'd taken his time with Escobar, played with Hollis's life. That was bad. But there was worse: he'd enjoyed it, had been excited by the power. The man he used to be, the man who'd built a home for his family, wouldn't have been capable of doing it. That man had been too soft.

'I ain't as soft as he was,' he said aloud.

He'd been soft when it came to saving Hollis's skin after they'd robbed the stage, and soft again when he agreed to take such good care of him.

'I should have asked for more money for doing it, I should have been harder,' he said.

Then he thought of Sarah. But the memories were confused and those that weren't were too painful. It was like walking in boots that pinched. So he thought about what he ought to be thinking about. What was he going to do now he'd got free of Hollis? Where would he head for? But every time he concentrated, his thoughts fought back. Think of a town, a territory, a state. One place seemed just as good as another. His thoughts were like wood shavings: when he tried to straighten them out, make them lie flat, they just slipped through his fingers and curled up into a springy spiral that would not be still.

He walked back to Billy's cabin. It was time to eat. But he wasn't hungry.

9

A Round Half-Dozen

Todd didn't sleep much. The wood shavings he tried to straighten wouldn't stop curling up again all night. Once, he thought he heard a noise outside.

The money!

He took a cautious peek out of the window. The moon was bright and he had a clear view of the bush and the picket fence. He saw no one. He stayed by the window for maybe an hour, gun in hand. There was no one there and he didn't hear the noise again. Must have been the wind, or some creek-water critter.

When it started to get light, he thought about going outside and moving the stash to a safer location. He wasn't really afraid for it. He just had a sudden hunger to get the money out and look at it.

He liked looking at it. It made him feel taller. But he resisted the temptation.

He'd been up an hour when Doc Halpern rode up. Sheriff Colhoun was with him.

Todd was immediately on his guard. What did they want? What did they know? But he rustled them up a pot of coffee, acted cheerful, behaved like he was real glad to see them.

'At least you're not missing or dead,' said the sheriff grimly. 'I was starting to worry about you too. One minute you and your pal — what was his name again . . . ?'

'Clarke. Hollis Clarke.'

' . . . one minute the pair of you are camped out at Ben Smiley's old place, the next there's no sign of you. And when a couple of Mexicans with guns hit town and start asking questions about where you might be, it's enough to make any man start wondering.'

'That was Escobar and Manolo,' Todd said casually. 'They were Hollis's friends, not mine. And not so much friends as associates. He had an idea for setting up a business importing Mexican goods. Hollis said they had the right contacts over the border.'

'So they'd be men of business, agents, go-betweens?'

'Reckon so. Hollis was going to put me in the picture but we ran into trouble and he got shot.'

'So you signed up with Hollis to some deal without knowing what it was?'

'Hollis is my friend, Sheriff. I trust him.'

'Is this business venture still a going concern?'

'Escobar caught up with us out at Ben's. We talked about the deal but decided not to do business with him after all.'

'So where'd he go?'

'He said back to Mexico,' said Todd.

'How long you have you known Hollis?'

'Met him during the war. We were in the same regiment. He saved my life once.'

It wasn't exactly true. Hollis had brought fresh ammo, that's all. If he hadn't, Todd would have slipped away when he'd fired his last shot and gone back to base. But saying he owed Hollis his life made it sound like they were blood brothers.

The sheriff thought about it.

'He just turned up one day,' Todd went on, filling the silence. 'Knew I was here because he found me through army records. It was just after the norther. I was pretty low. When he put the proposition to me, I leapt at it. It was like he was saving my life a second time' (which was true enough). 'I couldn't have stayed on the farm, putting it to rights again, there was no point. So just when I needed a new direction, good old Hollis showed up.'

'Where were you heading the day Hollis was shot?'

'Campo Largo. We were going to

meet Escobar there, fix up the details.'

'Who jumped you?'

'They didn't stop and give their names and we didn't ask,' said Todd ironically and immediately wished he hadn't: he'd told himself not to get smart. 'A bunch of *bandidos*. Looked like they'd just crossed the border. Didn't speak English. What's this all about, Sheriff?' said Todd, pretending to be more irritated than he was. 'You think I got my hands dirty?'

'Are you sure this Escobar wasn't one of the *bandidos*? Him and his sidekick looked less like go-betweens and more like tough hombres whose business was guns. Maybe you'd had that meeting you talked about and it went sour and your Mexican . . . associates decided to write the minutes with lead?'

'It happened like I told you,' said Todd, looking him in the eye like a man with nothing to hide. But all these questions were making him nervous. The sheriff looked at him for a moment, then said:

166

'When did you last see Mike Murphy?'

'The day of the norther, when he and Annie came round to see how I'd got on,' said Todd. 'And that's the last question I'm answering unless you tell me why you think I got something to do with Mike's disappearance.'

'No more questions. Anyway you got answers for everything,' said the sheriff. 'Thanks for the coffee.'

He stood up and left without saying another word.

When he'd gone, Todd said:

'What was that all about, Doc? He made me feel like a criminal. I ain't done nothing wrong.'

'I know that, Todd. You've always been straight as a die.'

'You said it,' said Todd Coulter, one of the good guys.

'Still, you can't blame Colhoun for thinking he can smell rotten fish. First Mike goes missing then there's no sign of you and Hollis. Next thing Escobar comes sniffing around town one day and suddenly he's got a couple of men in tow that looked like gunslingers. It didn't look good.'

'And where are they now?' asked Todd.

'Gone. No one seen hide nor hair of them either. What's got into people? Now you see them, now you don't. You've turned up, but Hollis hasn't.'

'Oh he's all right. He's up at the lake,' said Todd and immediately wished he hadn't.

'I thought you said he'd gone for good,' said the doc, with a furrow of the brow.

'He was at the lake when I left. He'll be gone by now.'

But he could tell the damage was done.

'And then there's two others haven't been seen. Charlie Denner and Abe Laufman. I'm surprised Colhoun didn't mention them.'

But the doc didn't expand. Instead he stood up and said it was time to go. He had calls to make.

'Was it a boy or a girl?' said Todd.

Doc Halpern looked puzzled.

'Last time, when you were out at Ben Smiley's, you said Mrs Chamberlain was due and Tom Fielding had broke his leg.'

'Girl,' said the doc with a smile, 'and all concerned doing just fine. Tom too.'

When he'd gone, Todd wondered if he'd done enough to cover up for his slip about Hollis being up at the lake. Maybe. But it was obvious Colhoun didn't think his story held up. And what was that crack about him having answers for everything? He'd just go on sniffing until he got a scent and when he did he'd follow it all the way.

On an impulse, Todd saddled up and rode out to Ben Smiley's place. The grave where they'd buried Mike was an empty hole. There was no body in it, no sign of a body anywhere nearby. Did the sheriff know about this? He looked again. The hole was ragged, untidy. It didn't look like it had seen a shovel. It could have been made by a coyote or maybe a wolf that had strayed down from the mountains. The thought of his friend being eaten by a wolf made him feel sick. He looked about him for anything that might show an animal was responsible. Nothing: it was too long since it had happened. But that in itself was a good sign. If Mike's body had been found, surely Annie would have known. There would have had to be a funeral — bodies didn't keep long in the summer heat. But the sheriff was a canny fellow. Maybe he knew Mick died with a bullet in him but not who put it there.

Making up his mind, he rode back to Cottonwood Creek, dug up his money, packed up the provisions he had bought and lit out for Leddy Lake to warn Hollis.

When he got there, Hollis was fishing off a rocky point directly in front of the lodge. Todd jumped off his horse which, tired after the journey, starting grazing.

'Didn't expect to see you again so soon,' said Hollis. 'What's wrong? You look like you ate a live frog.'

When Todd had told his story, Hollis asked:

'Who knows we're up here?'

'I told the sheriff and the doc that we'd split up, that you'd gone, for good.'

'We can't rule out that they'll come up here and look around. Maybe they'll also check with you out at the Creek. If they do, they'll find you've gone missing again. The sheriff was right about people disappearing right, left and centre.'

'It's not me I'm worried about. It's you. The sheriff has you down as the link. Wherever you've been, men have disappeared. And if he gets to you, he gets to me.'

'And he's right. Since we began all this, there's been a lot of killing. Too much. I never wanted it. Count them up: Paco, your friend Mike, Escobar, Manolo, those two gunslingers and the two guys from Clanton . . .'

'Denner and Laufman. That makes eight.'

'And the folks in town reckon I killed

them all?' said Hollis with a grin. 'My, I have been busy.'

'Look, I trailed all the way up here to warn you. I could have packed up and taken off some place far away where no one would know who I was.'

'Why didn't you?'

'We're friends. Friends are supposed to look out for each other.'

A bullet whipped the hat from his head. The crack of the rifle came a split-second later.

Todd leaped for cover, drawing his Colt as he ran. Hollis was a yard behind him. There were two more shots before they reached the lodge and threw themselves through the door. As they pulled it shut behind them, another bullet slammed into the wood.

Todd moved to the window and looked out.

'You see where the shots came from?'

'No,' said Hollis, 'but it was a rifle, not too close.'

'Close enough. Who the hell is shooting at us?'

'Whoever it was that followed you. You see anyone?'

'Come and take a look,' said Todd.

In just about the spot where Escobar had halted at the edge of the wood were now a couple of riders.

'Hey, gringo, you comin' out and we talk, no?'

'Paco!' said Hollis. 'So I didn't kill him after all!'

'Damn! I saw him yesterday! He was in the saloon in Clanton. I had him down for a cardsharp passing through. I didn't recognize him. No reason why I should, I only ever saw him once and then he was lying face down in the dirt after you'd shot him in the coach. But he had plenty of time to see me. When I walked into the saloon, he must have thought it was his birthday. He recognized me and followed me out to the Creek and then up here.'

'It don't matter. In a way I'm not sorry he's caught up with us. He's the one who started all this mayhem. It all began to go wrong after he winged me.

I should have finished him off myself on the road, when I had the chance. But I don't shoot defenceless men. Chivalry don't pay any more, though maybe it never did. Look where playing fair has got us! But this time, I'll do the job properly.'

But Todd wasn't listening.

'Where's my horse? It was grazing just by the point where you were fishing. The shots must have frightened it off. I can't see it anywhere.'

'Stop worrying, it'll come back.'

'Don't you get it?' yelled Todd. 'My money's in the saddle-bags!'

A bullet screamed through the window, narrowly missing his ear. He paid it no attention and blazed away through the broken glass until his Colt was empty.

'Get down!' snarled Hollis, 'you'll get yourself killed! Besides, we ain't got ammo to waste.'

Todd's legs gave way and he sat on the floor under the window with his back to the wall. His eyes were wild.

His money was out there! It was galloping around on the back of a frightened horse! He felt the loss like a pain. But Hollis went on yelling at him and slowly his breathing returned to normal.

'Hey, gringos! You comin' out, no?' shouted Paco. 'You give us money and we don' shoot no more!'

'Keep them covered,' said Hollis. 'I'm going out the back door, find out what's happening there.'

It didn't take long and the news wasn't good.

'They got us surrounded. You saw Paco and another guy out front. Well, there's another two out back. No way of walking away from this like we did last time, Todd. We have to fight it out.'

'But my money . . . ?'

'We'll get it back. And if we don't it won't make any odds, because we'll both be dead.'

Todd grunted and reloaded his gun.

'What they doing out back?' he asked.

'Nothing for now. Just keeping the place covered, one by the wood store and the other from the side of the stable.'

'We can't stay here. But how do we get out? They got the doors and windows covered. That leaves the roof. Or the chimney!'

The fireplace had been made of stone just like the one Todd had built in what seemed another life.

'I'll go,' said Todd. 'Don't want your wound opening up again. Besides, it was me who led them up here. And reason number three: my money's out there riding round on a horse. When I give the word, you create a diversion.'

He stood on the dead ashes of yesterday's fire, heaved himself up and started climbing. When his hands reached over the lip of the stack he gave Hollis the word.

'*Hola, Paco! Que tal, hombre?*' he heard him shout. 'How're you doing? Why are you shooting . . . ?'

Hoping that would be a sufficient

distraction, Todd pulled himself out on to the roof. His appearance was masked by the swaying of the dark foliage in the background. So far, so good. Moving as quietly as he could, he crawled to the overhang above the woodpile and looked down. A man was crouching, gun in fist, behind the heap of split logs directly below him. Without hesitation, Todd dropped boots first and landed on the back of the man's head. Before he could get up, Todd was on him. He grabbed a split log from the pile and slammed his man over the right ear. The man crumpled: he didn't move; he didn't even breathe.

Working his way along the cabin wall, Todd reached the end of it without attracting attention. He now had a clear view of the stable, a low building with stalls for just three horses, not more than ten yards away. Guarding the rear of the lodge, a swarthy man in a check shirt had his finger on the trigger of a rifle which pointed at the back door.

Todd hesitated. It was too far to try

and creep up on the man or rush him without being heard. He didn't want to use his gun because the shot would alert Paco. Treading as lightly as he could, he returned to the woodpile and gave a grunt of satisfaction. The axe was there, embedded in the block on which they split the logs. There was dried blood on the handle from the day Hollis had reopened his wound. He jerked it free, swung it in his hand to test the weight and balance and returned to the spot from where he could see the man with the rifle. He smiled. A rifle would make a welcome addition to their arsenal. Who in his right mind would bet sixguns against rifles?

Stepping out from the wall to give himself room, he raised the axe, took aim and threw it Indian fashion.

At the last moment, the man turned, warned by some instinct. But before he could turn his rifle on Todd, the axe caught him in the chest. Its weight slammed him against the wall of the stable and from there he bounced on to the ground. The axe was embedded in his chest as firmly as it had been in the wooden chopping-block just moments before.

Todd stood over him for a moment and watched the blood spread over the front of his check shirt which moved up and down four or five times, growing weaker each time until it stopped altogether.

That makes ten dead men, thought Todd — no, take away Paco who survived, so it makes nine, of which five are mine. He bent down, picked up the rifle, searched the man's pockets for extra shells and tapped quietly on the back door. When he heard a movement inside, he whispered to Hollis to open up.

'Two down, two to go,' said Todd. 'Next we take out Paco and his *amigo*.'

'We got to make this a close fight,' said Hollis. 'They got a rifle apiece and will pick us off if we give them a quarter of a chance. Paco's a pretty good shot.

Once I saw him hit a perched vulture at a hundred yards in a high wind. I say we split up. You go right, I go left and we'll come up behind them.'

'Agreed. But I get to take the rifle,' said Todd, unwilling to let Hollis have any advantage.

'You found it, you have it.'

They separated and crept through the undergrowth, slowly circling their opponents.

At first, Paco had gone on shouting for Hollis to come out. But when he got no answer and no further shots came from the lodge, he got suspicious. He told Diego, his sidekick, to scout round the back and find out what was happening from the two men he'd posted there. They weren't compatriots. He didn't trust *Americanos*, didn't like hiring them, but he'd had no choice. He'd been shot at close range. He'd been in no shape to send back home for *muchachos* with *cojónes* to hunt down the men who'd robbed Escobar. But now he'd found them, he'd soon get the money back. And maybe find out where Escobar had got to.

Paco went on sitting on his horse, watching the front of the lodge, waiting for Diego to return. All of a sudden, the front door burst open. Paco reached for his gun but pulled the shot wide when he saw it was Diego.

'*No están aqui! Los otros están muertos*!' he shouted. 'The gringos gone! The other *hombres* dead!'

Paco felt a cold sweat break out. He leaped off his horse and took cover behind a tree. How had the Americanos escaped? It was not possible! He'd had the house covered front and back. But escaped they had and that meant they were probably out here in the woods, maybe pointing a gun at him now! He looked nervously over his shoulder. Then he heard the crack of a rifle. He closed his eyes and braced himself for the impact. He opened them again and saw Diego, still on the stoop of the lodge, spin round, slam into the door jamb and collapse in a sprawl.

Suddenly the odds had changed and he didn't like them. His horse had shied when its rider had got off in a hurry and backed away again when Todd fired the shot that hit Diego. But it had not gone far. Paco decided it was time to get away. He made a run for it. He'd covered half the distance when Hollis stepped out of a bush pointing a gun at him.

Paco pulled up sharp.

'What happened to Juana?' asked Hollis in Spanish.

'Who?' said Paco, holding his hands in the air.

'Escobar's girl.'

'I tell you, you let me go?'

'Tell me now,' said Hollis and he shot Paco's left hand. Paco dropped on his knees nursing his hand which was now streaming with blood.

'I say again: what happened to Juana?'

Paco whimpered. Hollis fired again, this time into the sand by his left leg.

'Somebody hear her tokking how you

182

were goin' to steal Escobar's money. So he shot her.'

'How did he shoot her, Paco. Slowly? Like this?'

Another shot ripped into Paco's left knee. He howled.

'Take it easy, Hollis. This ain't a good idea.'

Todd had come to find out what all the shooting was about. He didn't like what he saw. He'd never seen his friend like this before.

'Or quick? Like this?'

He fired again. Paco's body twitched once and went still.

'That was for Juana,' said Hollis, holstering his gun.

Todd left him standing there, went into the stable, came out on Hollis's horse and returned half an hour later with his own.

There was now no bag hanging from the saddle.

In the lodge, Hollis was already halfway down a bottle of whiskey. Todd took a couple of slugs then left his friend to his thoughts.

He got out the small rowboat that was permanently moored to a flat rock which served as a jetty. The boat was weathered from under-use and water lollopped around his feet as he stepped into it. But it was serviceable. He gathered up the bodies, slung them over his horse one by one, and walked them down to the jetty. He threw each in turn into the bottom of the boat. He tied a rope around each neck. To the other end of the rope he attached a good-sized rock. Then one by one, four trips in all, he rowed the bodies out into the middle of Leddy Lake and dropped them over the side.

'That makes twelve dead men,' thought Todd grimly. 'A round dozen. And half of them are mine.'

Not bad for a beginner.

10

Plus One

When Todd got back to the lodge, the bottle had more or less the same amount of whiskey in it as when he went out. But if Hollis had stopped drinking and was less clenched and wound-up, Todd's mood, now that the action was over, was getting darker. Sinking bodies in a lake can have that effect. He poured himself a solid slug.

Hollis had been doing some serious thinking.

'That shoot-out don't change a thing, Todd, we're still in a fix,' he said. 'If Paco found us, then the sheriff will too. We can take it for granted he'll ride up here for a look-see. I would if I had his job. That's bad news for us both. You say

185

he's got me in his sights, but I guess he's none too sure about you either. We can't stay here.'

Todd didn't see it that way. The way he saw it Colhoun was convinced Hollis was guilty of murder, but Todd felt he himself was in the clear, or at least there was nothing against him that would stick. Anyway, this whole sorry mess was all Hollis's fault. It was Hollis who'd got him into it, Hollis who'd started the killing. He wished he'd never signed up for the deal, a disaster from the start. But since he'd come this far, and had a pile of money buried in the woods, there was no sense throwing it all away by backing down now. He'd earned that money.

'If you say so. But we don't go together. We go separate ways.'

'Fair enough. But I'm not going down the mountain and risk meeting the sheriff coming up. I'm going over the Knuckle and out the back way.'

'I'll go back to Clanton. They got nothing they can pin on me. You and me just got to the end of the road, Hollis.'

'I never wanted it to end like this, old friend . . . '

'Don't give me that. You just wanted a patsy on tap because you couldn't work the Escobar job by yourself.'

'You're wrong, Todd . . . '

'All that old pals talk and how you was going to let me in on a good thing . . . '

Todd felt his anger rising. If he was up at Leddy Lake, on the run, with six notches on the butt of his gun and a pile of money which he couldn't spend and had buried and dug up more times than he could count, he wasn't to blame, not for any of the mess.

' . . . and all I've had is running round after you: wipe your nose, fetch and carry, do this, do that. Well, old friend,' he sneered bitterly, 'I turned into a killer thanks to you. And I was the one who's had to take questions from the doc and have Colhoun interrogate me while you sat up here fishing! Fishing!'

'Hold it, Todd. You're running on ahead of yourself. We started this together, and we'll finish it on a handshake, with no hard feelings. If you want to go your way, go.'

'I don't need your permission to do anything! I'm not taking any more orders from you. I'm through.'

And he stormed out, slamming the door behind him. He strode angrily down to the lake and stared out across the flat, unruffled water. Sarah had swum from this point; he'd dived off that rock. Then they'd gone back to the lodge and made love. As his mind filled with those good times, his anger continued to rise. Goddammit! What had he ever done to deserve this? How come everything he'd tried to build up had been knocked down?

His anger slowly turned to rage. He hated the insolent calm of the lake, the softness of the air, the green of the hills reflected in the water. But most of all he hated Hollis.

He turned and was in time to see the man he'd once called friend come out from behind the lodge leading his horse which was saddled up and ready to go. It hadn't taken him long, thought Todd who all of a sudden found himself running towards the lodge. When he was ten yards away, Hollis turned and saw him. On his face was that insufferable, superior grin.

Without breaking his stride, Todd slammed straight into him. Hollis was driven back against his horse which shied away and he fell heavily to the ground. Todd staggered, lost his balance and finished on his back. Hollis sat up:

'What the blazes you playing at, Todd?'

But Todd was on his feet and coming towards him. He aimed a kick at Hollis's head but Hollis grabbed his leg and pulled him off balance again.

'This ain't how friends is supposed to part,' he said.

'You ain't no friend of mine,' snarled Todd who jumped up and came on again.

Hollis stuck out a left. There was no

power in it because he wasn't sure what was happening. If it was just a matter of Todd taking his frustration on the nearest thing that moved, he could understand, and he wasn't going to hand out any lessons in fist-fighting. Todd replied with a haymaking right which missed by a whisker.

'Cool off!' said Hollis, retreating from a flurry of blows.

This time Todd did not answer and by the gleam in his eye Hollis knew he was in a real fight. He stopped retreating and squared up.

He stuck out another left which caught Todd on the side of the head but did little damage. Todd swung at him again but missed with another right, which also hit only thin air. The momentum carried him forward. Hollis stepped back and chopped him with a right over the ear. Todd tottered, regained his balance and shook his head to clear it.

'Cut it out,' said Hollis, 'there's no need for this.'

But he no longer recognized the man facing him. His face was dark with rage and his breath came in short, angry rasps. He was in no mood to listen to reason and Hollis gave up trying.

On came Todd, swinging wildly. Hollis stood back from him and when Todd overreached himself, peppered him with lefts to his face. With one hook he split an eyebrow and with an uppercut to the chin rocked Todd back on his heels. He followed up with a solid right to the heart and a vicious bola punch which doubled him up. Todd dropped his hands.

But instead of wading in to finish off his man, Hollis stepped back.

'Stop this now, or one of us ain't going anywhere. So you don't want us to ride together any more. That's fine by me. You got your money, I got mine, we're quits. Why not leave it at that?'

Quits! Todd couldn't believe his ears! How could he ever be quits with a man who'd lured him away from the Todd Coulter everyone knew for a straight sort of fellow and turned him into a desperado with six notches on his gun-butt? 'I ain't that good old Todd Coulter,' he told himself, 'no more than he's the Hollis Clarke I knew in the army. Bad things had happened to Hollis that had changed him that weren't his fault. But they'd made him mean and vicious. And the badness has infected me. Me? I shot men in the war. That was duty. Lately, I killed lots of men and I liked it. I'm a regular killing machine. He made me one. But I want it to stop now and there's only one way of doing that: root out the source of the evil.'

He came on again, shaking his head and with blood streaming from his cut eyebrow. Throwing punches and absorbing everything that was thrown at him, he forced his opponent on to the back foot. With a scything left hook he clipped Hollis on the chin, but in return he took a solid right to the nose. It was not strong enough to break it, but it made it bleed and the blood got in the way of his breathing. Hollis danced away and Todd, frustrated by the way his target ducked and weaved, snorted like an enraged bull, got more furious and advanced in grim pursuit.

Then Hollis changed tactics. He stood his ground and, cooler headed, put together combinations of lefts and rights which left Todd dazed and reeling. Switching his attack to the body, he repeated the treatment. Todd dropped his arms and he started to blow.

Hollis moved in for the finish; Todd straightened up for one last effort.

He traded blows for a moment but took more good shots than he gave. He stood a pace back, sank into a crouch and ran at Hollis, grabbing him around the waist, pulling him to the ground where he wouldn't be able to jig and dance. Hollis was carried back four or five paces before Todd's weight slammed him against the rail of the stoop and then both of them were rolling in the dirt.

Todd was again the first to recover. He got on his knees and straddled his opponent who put up no resistance. His eyes were closed and he'd gone slack. Hollis was out of it.

Todd rolled off him and lay panting on his back looking up at the sky until his breathing returned to normal. He stood up, took Hollis's gun in case he woke up, and walked slowly down to the edge of the lake. There he bathed his faced, held his burning, skinned knuckles in the cool water and sat until his thoughts had reached the same even rhythm as his breathing.

His rage had subsided completely and he felt drained and very foolish. What had got into him? Hollis was a regular guy. He'd always been straight, never tried to welsh on him. But something had snapped. 'I got to control myself,' he muttered. 'How come I thought it was all rough seas for me, plain sailing for him? Look at the facts. He's come off worse twice: once shot and now unconscious.' But at least one thing was clear, he thought ruefully, fingering his nose: Hollis had given him a pretty good whipping and he deserved it.

He walked back to the lodge. Hollis was still out. Blood had soaked in the dust under his head. It came from the cut above his left ear which he had got when his head had cannoned against the corner of the deck of the stoop. Todd fetched water from the lake and poured it on Hollis's face. He fetched the whiskey bottle and tried in vain to get some down his throat. In the end, Todd decided to leave him to come to in his own time. Hollis, he knew from the old days, had a skull like a rock.

He sat on the stoop, took out the makings and rolled up a cigarette. After a while, he started to get restless. If Hollis was right and the sheriff might put in an appearance at any moment, maybe it was time to go. But he couldn't leave Hollis like this.

It was as he stepped off the porch that he saw the blood that had trickled out of Hollis's ear and realized that his friend wasn't breathing. His skin was already cool to the touch and when Todd raised one of his arms, it flopped like a dead weight.

'He can't do this to me!' said Todd, and he felt the anger swell again. He fought it, but it rose again when he mentally added another notch to his tally. Seven! How did I ever manage to kill seven men?

He suddenly felt very small under a very big sky. He was in a jam — his so-called friend's parting shot, he thought bitterly — and needed to do some fast thinking.

He had to get away from the lodge. But he couldn't leave Hollis dead on the stoop. Only he knew Hollis was up at Leddy Lake and no one ever came here this time of year. So he'd be the main suspect. He couldn't bury him anywhere near. The sheriff might look around and sniff out a grave. Anyway, hadn't Mick given him proof that bodies don't always stay buried for long in these parts? Damn Hollis!

And then there was the small matter

of Hollis's money. He wouldn't be needing it anymore and it made no sense just to leave it in a hole in the ground to moulder. Hollis would surely want him to have it? He'd been all packed up to leave. But there was no money-bag on his horse. That meant he probably hadn't hidden it anywhere near and was counting on retrieving it somewhere along his trail, the trail leading up and over The Knuckle. That meant it could be anywhere! Todd decided there was no point even in thinking about looking for it unless he wanted to dig holes everywhere and turn the whole valley into a rabbit warren. He'd have to make do with his share. Damn Hollis! He went on causing trouble even after he was dead.

What were the priorities? First, to get away from here; second, to take Hollis with him; third, to look out for Hollis's money.

He slung Hollis over his saddle and tied his hands to his feet under the horse's belly. He covered up the blood in the dirt and sluiced down the edge of the stoop. He took a last look around the lodge and the stables to make sure he'd left no tell-tale traces of the battle they'd fought earlier with Paco or of which way he'd gone. He fetched a shovel from the stables — he couldn't bury a body with his bare hands — and strapped it to his horse. He hitched the rein of Hollis's mount to his saddle and rode slowly through the shallow water of the lakeshore so as to leave no tracks. Once he stopped, to rescue his money from the hole in the split-trunk tree, where he had hidden it when he'd gone to fetch his horse which had been frightened away by the shooting.

There was only one way to go. He could not risk heading back towards Clanton and bumping into Colhoun. What would he say? 'Glad to meet you, Sheriff. Look, I got a body for you. It's my old army friend. Sure I was the only one knew he was here, except you and the doc . . . ' He'd take his chances with the Knuckle.

The light was going by the time he reached the end of the lake. It wasn't a good idea to go further in the gathering dark so he decided to stop for the night. He lifted Hollis off his horse and laid him on the ground. Maybe he should bury the body here. Best not. Any hunters and fishermen who came up to Leddy Lake now were likely to use this trail. Safest was to take Hollis up to the terrace where they'd left Escobar. No one went there any more, guaranteed. He wrapped the body in a blanket, rustled up a bite to eat and settled down for the night.

He didn't sleep. His bruised face throbbed and Sarah was not pleased with him.

At first light, he sluiced water over his swollen face and set out just as the first rays of the sun hit the western shore of the lake.

An awkward three-hour ride — Hollis's horse now decided it didn't like carrying a corpse and jibbed when it thought about it — brought him to the old mine workings.

Everything looked just as it had when he and Hollis had fought it out with Escobar. But the tunnel at the far end had fallen in. The bodies were where they had dumped them, under a pile of rocks deep in the first mine shaft; there was a smell of decomposition in the dank air. When he struck a match, he saw that the rocks had been no defence against the local rats.

He went out into the sunshine and stood there a moment, blinking until his eyes grew accustomed to the glare. The terrace looked the same, but a few more big boulders had fallen from higher up. A couple of hundred feet above his head, a long finger of rock pointed up at the sky. That's where you get fingers, he thought: on a knuckle. The stones had come from there. In fact, the cliff face looked flaky which was all to the good. The threat of rocks calving off it would keep nosey-parkers from getting too close.

He walked the length of the terrace,

casting around for a suitable spot to dig a decent grave for Hollis. It was the least he could do for a man who, if he faced the truth, had been the only true friend he'd ever had.

He couldn't leave Hollis to the rats that lived in the disused workings. At the far end of the terrace, recent rains — which probably helped explain why the tunnel had collapsed — had gouged scars deep enough to make Todd think that even if Meacher and the gunman hadn't set off the scree slide, it would have happened sooner or later all by itself, by the force of gravity. He climbed down to a likely looking rock, firmly planted in a gentle slope where the grass grew lush in the good earth. Below, the western end of the lake gleamed in the sunshine. This was where Hollis would rest in peace.

He climbed back up, fetched the horses and picketed them. He took the shovel, scrambled back down to the rock and started digging.

11

Colour!

When Hollis was safely under six feet of earth and loose rock, Todd covered the place with the green turves he'd dug out for the hole, stamped them flat, rested on his shovel for a few minutes and then climbed back up to the terrace.

The sun was setting. He picked out a fresh tunnel and got a fire going in the mouth of it. After he'd eaten, he sat thinking. Tomorrow, he'd say goodbye to Leddy Lake and Clanton and Hamilton County and vanish over the Knuckle and off the face of the earth.

He reached for his saddle bags and took out his money. He laughed to see how golden the bundles looked in the last rays of the sun. He counted the bundles and marvelled again at how many dollars could be fitted into so small a bag.

While there was still light, he packed it away, spread his blanket on the floor of the tunnel and laid out his money bag for his head. Before settling down for the night, he stood a couple of dead, dry, thorny branches across the mouth of the tunnel which anyone trying to get in could not pass without making a noise. Then he laid himself down.

He fell asleep instantly. Suddenly, he was awake. He couldn't tell how long he had been in dreamland, for the night was moonless. His eyes were open and his senses on full alert. What had he heard? The thorn barrier? He sat up, gun in hand. Twice he heard noises. The first might have been a boot scraping a rock, and the second like something had been dropped. He did not venture outside. He had no intention of being an easy target for anyone.

'They won't get me that easy,' he thought grimly.

At first light, he stood up and peered

out cautiously. Everything looked as it had the night before, except that one arm of the thorn barricade had moved. Or had been moved. He saw no footmarks but thought he could make out the traces of a small animal. He relaxed. That might account for the noises he'd heard in the night. But maybe not.

He caught a movement out of the corner of one eye which proved to be the branch of a tree swaying in the wind. He jumped when a crow cawed somewhere up on the cliff face way above his head. He told himself he mustn't get jittery, that there was no one around.

Except for Hollis.

Hollis! Maybe he wasn't dead! Maybe he'd been shamming!

He reached for the shovel, slithered down to where he'd buried the body. It all looked just as he'd left it. But that didn't mean a thing. The grave could have been put back to look exactly as it was. He couldn't take any chances. He tore the turves away and removed the earth and rocks that covered the body. He almost sobbed with relief when at last his shovel met something soft: Hollis's waistcoat. He scraped away the earth from Hollis's face, just to be sure it was him, then started to cover him up again.

Wait a moment. Maybe this was a bad spot for a grave. It was only a few yards below the lip of the terrace. It was visible from above and very accessible. He had to find a better place for it.

Leaving the grave open, he climbed back up and explored the area beyond the point where the terrace ended. A faint animal track led him along a narrower ledge to a low bank above which grew a dense, spiky-leafed bush. He climbed up and decided he'd found the right place.

He went back for Hollis, hauled him up to the low bank and left him there. He returned for the shovel and started digging under the spiky bush. He'd got down two feet and was finding the going surprisingly easy, as if the earth had been dug up recently, when his shovel met something that wasn't hard, like a root or a rock, but refused to give the shovel best. He put the shovel down and started digging with his hands. It took him only a few minutes to uncover the obstacle which proved to be a leather bag. It looked like the one Hollis had used. He opened it. It was full of bundles of money.

'This is my lucky day!' he said and gave a great whoop which scattered the birds in the trees nearby.

He understood. Hollis had decided to go over the Knuckle. So instead of burying his money near the lodge where he couldn't get it fast if he needed to make a quick getaway, which he would if Colhoun should drop by unexpectedly for a chat, he'd brought it up here so he could pick it up on his way over the Knuckle. So Hollis had had the same idea about finding a safe place to hide it and had ended up with the very spot Todd had chosen to bury him in.

He couldn't wait to pull all the bundles out and count them and check it was all there and add the money to his own. But he mastered his impatience and went on digging out Hollis's new resting place.

From time to time he stopped to wipe the sweat out of his eyes and each time he could not help laughing. Must be a nervous reaction, he thought, and then started laughing uncontrollably again.

At last the hole was long and deep enough. He hauled Hollis up and rolled him into it. He covered him with earth, brushed the dirt on the top of the grave with a bushy branch to cover all trace of its existence and slid back down the slope with Hollis's bag held firmly in one hand. He shouldered it and returned along the narrow ledge. He sat in his tunnel, spread Hollis's bundles on the ground and counted them. Ten thousand bucks! It was all there. He particularly liked the bundle of twenties. He got his own money out and laid it out next to Hollis's heap and sat back with a satisfied sigh. He remained there for some time just for the pleasure of looking at twenty thousand dollars. Not just any twenty thousand: his twenty thousand.

Suddenly he was aware that it was late. No sense in trying to cross the mountain now — that would be asking for trouble. It was going to be hard enough traversing the terrain on the other side and it made no sense to make difficulties. So he put Hollis's money back in his friend's bag, returned his own money to his and hid both of them ten yards inside the tunnel under a heap of spoil that had fallen from the roof. Then he went out to water the horses and refill his canteen from the stream he'd used the last time he was here. He was thirsty. It had been a busy day.

He walked to the end of the terrace, climbed down past the spot where he'd buried Hollis the first time and started down towards the stream. Maybe his mind was still on all that money, maybe the light was fading faster than he'd expected and made him underestimate the pitch of the slope. But he suddenly lost his footing and found himself careering down the hillside. He tried to grab saplings and clumps of bushes but succeeded only in scorching his hands. He felt himself gathering speed and tried to dig his heels in, for a brake. And then, without warning, there was nothing under his heels, nothing under his body, nothing for his hands to clutch at and he was in freefall. He bounced off a rock and was brought up short in a rattle of small stones. They sounded like dead men's fingers playing a tattoo on his skull.

That pattering rhythm, which grew fainter, was the last thing he heard until he opened his eyes again. For a moment, he didn't know where he was or how long he'd been there. He couldn't see a thing; there was nothing to hear, except silence. Then he remembered, but it wasn't remembering that made his head ache.

He tried moving his arms. He found he could do so if he made a big effort. The same with his legs. As far as he could tell, nothing was broken but he felt like he was pinioned, trapped, like Gulliver in the book. That was also why he couldn't sit up.

He tried to marshal his thoughts. While he did so, the blackness around him slowly turned a kind of milky grey. He had a raging thirst and his tongue had become too big for his mouth which tasted of blood. When he moved, the dead men rattled their fingers again. He tried to lift his arms. They rattled some more. He had a feeling that their grip was slacker. He moved his legs and then his arms again, all with the dead men rattling their fingers, and soon he had extricated himself from the loose scree that had half buried him. Now he remembered.

He'd lost his footing and slid down the mountain, how far he didn't know. He ached everywhere but he didn't think he was seriously injured.

He tried to sit up. The effort made his stomach heave but soon his head cleared and he began to feel better. He sat without moving for a few minutes, waiting a spell before trying again. While he waited, the light grew stronger. He craned his head back and looked up. Above him, not more than fifteen feet away, was a slit filled with newly-washed blue sky. He reckoned he was in a crevasse. He made a mighty effort and stood up.

He leaned against the wall at his back for support. His head swam again. When the world stopped spinning, he saw rock in front of him, six or seven feet away. Over the ages, the scree under his boots had filled the split in the mountain. If it hadn't, he'd have fallen a lot further.

Even so, he still had to get out of the hole he'd landed in. The lip of the crevasse was out of his reach and the walls crumbled when he tried to find a hand hold.

In the strengthening light, he saw

that the crevasse was not straight but turned a few yards further along to his left. Perhaps there was a way out around that corner. Cautiously, fearing a wrong step might trigger the scree which, seeking its own level like water, might give way and send him plunging into unseen depths. He reached the corner safely and peered round it.

Yesterday had truly been his lucky day. He'd found Hollis's money, he'd taken a bad fall without breaking anything and he had lived to tell the tale. But if that was good luck, it was nothing compared to what happened to him now.

Straight ahead was a vertical seam of quartz. It was veined with gold. Small gold nuggets dotted the scree at the foot of the rock wall where they had fallen out of the quartz. He'd heard old-time miners talking about the time they'd found colour. He knew exactly how they felt.

When he'd got over the first shock, he picked up a few of the nuggets and examined them. He'd heard all about fool's gold, but he knew enough about rocks to tell that this was the real thing. The rocks all round were exactly the right rocks for gold-bearing ores. No wonder miners had chosen this spot on the mountain to try their luck. With his knife he stabbed at the quartz. It crumbled easily and as it crumbled, it released more gold. The vein disappeared into the ground beneath his feet. It might peter out quickly or it might go a long way down. It was too soon to tell. But the signs were good. He was already looking at a fortune.

He felt weak-kneed, though whether it was from the fall or on account of being faced by such awesome good fortune he couldn't have said. But one thing was very clear to him: a man with twenty thousand dollars in cash and a virgin gold strike could call himself very rich without fear of contradiction.

But a man in his predicament also had to admit he was in a hole.

Carefully he retraced his steps until he was standing under the mouth of the crevasse. The rock face crumbled dangerously. But by cutting deeper with his knife, he found he could make hand- and footholds which took his weight. Twice they didn't and he fell back heavily. The scree shook but held. He tried again. In the end, he reached over the top and found a tree root which he used to haul himself up into the sunlight. He lay on his back, panting with the effort.

His terrifying slide had taken him no more than fifty yards down the mountain. But the angle was fierce, the going treacherous and it took some climbing to get back to level ground. On the way, he found his canteen dangling where it had caught on a tree branch. He filled it from the fast-flowing stream. He drank deeply and felt refreshed. He was aware that he was very hungry. He remembered he'd had no supper.

His tunnel on the terrace had not

been disturbed overnight. The money was still where he'd hidden it.

He ate, replaced the thorn barricade and slept like a man with no troubles.

12

Paytime

Next morning, he sat on a rock on the terrace cradling a tin cup of coffee and took stock.

Making that strike had changed everything. No way could he get on his horse and head out over the Knuckle and abandon what had cost him so much to get. If a man was being hunted, he wouldn't think twice: he'd take his chances with the wilderness. But a man with twenty thousand dollars cash and a goldmine in his pocket had no call to run. Now Hollis was dead, he could take all the blame. Colhoun had nothing he could pin on Todd so there was no reason why he should run scared. Conclusion: he'd go back to Clanton, bide his time, and work out the best way to become what he was: a rich man. Then he'd be safe. A rich man can always buy himself out of trouble.

He was surprised he didn't feel bad about ending up with Hollis's half of the money. It was Hollis who had dragged him down, so it was only right that he should get his share. It was blood money. It wiped the slate clean.

But not his hands.

But if he was going back to Clanton, he'd have to hide the money again. No good leaving the bags under a pile of rocks in the tunnel. The rats would gnaw through the leather and dine out for weeks on all those crisp bills.

After a morning spent looking, he found a cleft in a rock which he sealed with two heavy stones. There it would stay hidden from the weather, animals and prying eyes. Before he told it goodbye, he took a bundle of ones and another of fives. It should be enough to tide him over until he was in a position to return and reclaim his fortune.

Before leaving, he ate again. Then he scattered the ashes from his fire and left his tunnel looking as if no one had been in it for years.

He saddled his horse and led Hollis's. He didn't like the idea of shooting it, but he could hardly leave it to roam and perhaps be recognized. If a search was organized for Hollis, it could create problems. So half way down the mountain, he found a sort of natural quarry where he put his Colt into the horse's ear and pulled the trigger. He disposed of the saddle in the lake outflow which swept it away.

The lodge was exactly as he had left it. He stopped off briefly to check it out again for anything that might incriminate him and rode on, though not before looking across at the Knuckle and giving it, his money and Hollis his crispest military salute.

The heat of the plain seemed oppressive after the coolness of the high mountain. He paused briefly to look down on the Murphy farmstead which fitted into a gentle dell snug as a bullet in a gun barrel. No smoke showed at the chimney of the house and no animals grazed in the fields. Annie must still be staying with Billy Stephens' sister.

He had not seen his own place since the day of the norther. The wreckage which had remained in his memory as stark and sharp in outline had been blurred and greened by a new growth of weeds. Weeds were even sprouting between the stone of the chimney he had built. In the twilight, he watered and picketed his horse which started feeding on the lush grass that had quickly taken hold. Nature never stops: it finds a bare patch and moves in to fill it. He collected enough broken spars of wood to make a fire. He ate. Then he stretched out, rolled a smoke and watched the stars until his eyelids came down on them.

Next morning he rode into town. In his pocket he carried half a bundle of dollar bills.

'Dang me if it isn't Jumping Jack turned up again,' cried Jim Hicks with a grin. 'I sure am glad to see you. Folks have been worrying. So, what can I do for you.'

'Provisions, but I also want some tools. I lost mine in the norther. I'm going back to my place. Do it up. Make a new start.'

While Hicks started filling his order, Todd picked out what he needed by way of tools and walked over to the stables where he rented a cart from Hank Beynon to transport his goods. He was driving back to Hicks's store when the sheriff stepped out of his office.

'Heard you was in town,' he said. 'I thought you'd done another vanishing trick. I trailed all the way out to Cottonwood Creek. When I got there, the place was deserted.'

'Yep, I moved out,' said Todd who, mindful of watching his manners and of saying and doing the right thing, added: 'But first things first. Any news of Mick?'

'Nothing. But it don't look good. It's been a long time and the chances of him being alive are pretty small. Not that I'd tell Annie that. So if you see her, remember to stay cheerful.'

'Sure will. Sorry if I gave you a nasty moment, but I've been back at my own place, doing a spot of planning. After you and the doc left that day, I got to thinking. That norther flattened more than my farm: it flattened me too. But Sarah wouldn't have wanted me to spend the rest of my life fretting, being angry, moving from one place to the next. So I decided to go back . . . home' — the hesitation was momentary — 'fix it up, bring it back to life. I think it's what Sarah would have wanted me to do.'

He spoke glibly, almost without thinking about what he was saying. He was amazed how easily the lies came. In the old days, the Todd Coulter he'd been could never have lied like that.

When he got back to the farm, he unloaded his supplies and equipment and smoked a cigarette.

Sarah said: 'You sure pulled the wool over the sheriff's eyes! I was real proud of you back there! Now Hollis is out of the way, you're in charge. That's good. You're doing everything right. The money's safe, the heat's off, Colhoun don't suspect a thing. Only fly in the ointment is that now you have to start fixing the place up. The waiting won't be easy. Still, working on the house will give you something to do.'

Todd made a start on cleaning up the mess, salvaging what he could and stacking it neatly for re-use, and putting splintered puncheons and logs to one side for burning. He rode up into the woods and earmarked trees for felling. He drove stakes into the ground and replaced lengths of the picket fence. He hauled logs, trimmed them and laid them over the foundations of the cabin the norther had blown down.

A couple of times Doc Halpern dropped by. Todd never offered him liquor, only coffee. But he himself began drinking. He did not drink to get drunk nor did he ever get drunk. He drank just enough to take the edge off his sombre moods, to dull his impatience and blunt his anger against the world's injustice. Some nights, when he couldn't sleep, he felt gnawed at by guilt. When it got bad, when the booze didn't dull or numb or take the edge off it, he would step outside and shout at the stars: 'I killed seven men!' and recite all their names, always ending 'and the last was Hollis Clarke, my friend!'

There was no one to hear him.

The work gave him something to do, but it didn't occupy his mind. The waiting got him down. He would sit smoking on a log and lie awake at night thinking about the money. He remembered what it looked like when the bundles were arranged in patterns. He remembered what it felt and smelled like and the whirring sound it made, like a locust's wings, when he riffled a bundle. He wished it were nearby so he could take it out and look at it. In his mind he conjured up memories of the crevasse, of his wall of gold, the complex tracery of gold veins in the quartz, as beautiful as if they'd been hung there by a golden spider or painted by the world's greatest artist.

When he'd stopped thinking about the nuggets lying on the floor like lumps of common stone, he imagined the things that wealth could do for him. He could go anywhere, do whatever he wanted, buy anything. There'd be travel in trains, the best horses to ride, women and card games and, if he wanted it, a future as a businessman doing deals, overpowering his rivals with the power of his money. He might even buy himself public office, maybe even run for senator.

But he could do none of these things yet. He would have to wait. It was as if his money was in prison, serving a long sentence, waiting to be released so that his new life could begin at last. At other times, he thought it was like a fiddle shut up in its case where it couldn't play tunes. His money was soundless music. It was as close to him, and as faraway, as Sarah.

At intervals of two or three weeks, he rode into Clanton to stock up. While he was there, he'd take a drink or two in the saloon. He would stand, one boot on the foot rail, and look into the back bar mirror. It was here that it began, when Hollis appeared out of the blue and turned his life upside down, rerouted it along a wide money trail that seemed to have no ending. He would smile at the thought that now the end was in sight.

It was also here that he saw Paco and the number seven would come into his mind.

One day, as he walked into the stores, always his first port of call, Jim Hicks said: 'Doc Halpern's left a message for you. You're to go to his house the moment you get here. Urgent. Don't go anywhere else first. He was very insistent about that.'

Todd sauntered over to the doc's, wondering what all the fuss was about.

The doc himself opened the door.

'Come in,' he said, almost yanking Todd across the threshold. He shut the door quickly.

'Anyone see you?' he said.

'Only Hicks. He gave me your message. What's all this about? Why so mysterious?'

'Come through.'

The doc led him into his surgery and sat him down. Then he perched on the edge of his bureau, swinging his leg.

'I always had a lot of time for you, Todd. A good man through and through. But there's a rumour going round that don't put you in a very good light. I'd like to hear what you got to say about it.'

'What rumour?'

'I don't know if you ever met Teddy Woods and his boy Tom? No? Sheepmen both, the old school. Every spring they march the flock up into the mountains to their summer pasture and in late autumn they bring them down again for the winter. They're a couple of weeks early this year on account of the rains. It's been torrential up there, Teddy said, water everywhere. Anyways, he's back now until the Spring. He says he had a trip back down to Clanton about halfway through the summer, he reckons, to stock up at Hicks's store. He filled his cart and set off back. But instead of taking the direct route, he made a detour and went past Ben Smiley's place. He always did that, to see if Ben was around — Teddy and Ben go back a long way. He wasn't clear about exact dates but it must have been around the early part of August. That was about when you were there with Hollis, I guess.'

'About then, yes,' said Todd, a mild feeling of panic tightening his stomach.

'You ever see anything of Teddy? Old feller, long moustache all yellowed with that God-awful tobacco he smokes?'

'Never saw anybody like that. Mind, I wasn't at Smiley's place all the time. I don't recall Hollis ever mentioning anybody of that description.'

'The point is that when he passed Ben's place on his way back up the mountain, he reckoned the place was occupied.'

'That'll have been us.'

'He said he saw Mick ride in. He was about to follow, thinking old Ben was back, when he heard shots, maybe two, he couldn't tell for sure. He kept his head down and waited to see what happened next. But he never saw Mick come out, but there could have been lots of reasons for that. Nothing bad seemed to be happening and he didn't want to barge in and find they'd been shooting rats. Besides, he had to get back up that mountain before it got dark. So he lit out. It's only now that he's told Sheriff Colhoun the story.'

'What does the sheriff make of it?'

'He went straight out to the Smiley place soon as he heard what Teddy Woods had to say, to look around.'

'And you?' asked Todd. 'What do you reckon to what Teddy Woods says he saw?'

The doc shrugged. 'The sheriff got back and went straight round to Billy's sister's house to see Annie with a piece of check shirt and a boot he found in the scrub at the back of the cabin. Annie recognized them, said they were Mick's for sure. What I think is what everybody thinks: Mick was murdered. That's as far as I've got.'

'If it was about August, Hollis was still nursing that wound. He was there all the time. Me, I came and went. This is the first I heard of it.'

'Maybe, but this looks bad for you, Todd. There's no other way I can put it.'

'But it don't make sense. I liked Mick. He and Annie were real good to me. Why should I want to kill him?'

The doc didn't answer.

'Why are you telling me this, Doc?'

'Like I said, I don't have you down for a bad man. But good people sometimes do bad things, not because they want to but because they're forced into it. If you've done something bad, I know you didn't intend to. So I'm giving you a chance to put it right.'

'You mean own up to something I never did just so the sheriff can get his man, the law can hang a murderer and the people of Clanton can sleep safe in their beds again?' said Todd, getting to his feet, breathing injured innocence. 'I've got nothing to hide, but I ain't going to stick around for Colhoun to put a noose around my neck. If anybody wants me, I'll be out at my place. I got a roof to put on my house.'

Todd left town knowing the game was up. He rode back fast to the farm, strapped on his gun, filled an old sack with supplies and headed straight back up the mountain. He wouldn't hide. He wouldn't try to hole up on the terrace. He'd dig up the money, go over the Knuckle and disappear into the wilderness. He'd figure out later what to do about the strike.

From time to time he turned and looked over his shoulder.

As he rode, the irony of it all struck

him with the weight of a punch to the gut. He had killed seven men. And here he was, accused of a murder he hadn't committed! It took his breath away. Hollis was having the last laugh from beyond the grave. But it wasn't just Hollis, it was the sun, moon and stars and whatever it was that made it all go round by toying with men, fixing the odds, rigging the game. It was one enormous, universal farce, and the joke was on him.

The lake was fuller than when he'd seen it last. Teddy Woods was right. Everywhere was wet. A tree had blown down just beyond the lodge and he had to keep making big detours to avoid areas of marsh he had previously known as firm going. His horse left big, messy tracks in the soggy earth that no one could miss. But given where he was going, he didn't care.

The rise in the level of lake water had turned the outflow into a torrent. He dismounted, leading his horse, crossed it with great difficulty and got a thorough soaking for his pains.

As he gained height, he paused in places where the far bank of the lake was visible. At first he saw nothing. Then he thought he glimpsed movement. He pressed on. From the next vantage point he had a clear sighting of a group of riders: it could only be the sheriff with a posse. They had found his trail.

The higher the trail climbed, the more it deteriorated. The rains had scooped out deep channels across it and washed it away in parts. Twice, the weight of water had caused a small landslip which needed great care to cross safely. But though his progress was slow, he rose steadily higher and higher and at last approached the terrace.

He and his horse were tiring when at last he saw the cleft rock with the sapling growing out of it. A few yards more, get round the rock and the terrace would be there, waiting. He wasn't worried that his pursuers would be gaining on him, for they'd be finding the going hard too. He'd have plenty of time to dig up the money and be gone before the leading riders reached the terrace.

'Still one step ahead of the opposition', Sarah said in his ear, 'still winning. You've seen off Hollis, the Mexicans, everybody who got in your way. Shame about Mick. But he shouldn't have come poking his busybodying nose in where it wasn't wanted. You've been through the mill, Todd. You deserve to win, you've earned it'.

He picked his way carefully round the split rock and came to a dead stop.

There was no more trail. There was no terrace. The slope on which it had perched was a scar of exposed earth. The rains had washed away the teetering finger of rock, the cliff honeycombed with tunnels and shafts, the broad terrace and everything else. The whole mountainside had been scraped bare. The bodies of Escobar and his men were gone. Hollis had been swept away and the money with him and the crevasse with the wall of gold had been buried under a tide of mud.

At first he couldn't take it in. It was not possible. Then he saw that it was not only possible but had happened. He was filled with rage and he brandished his fist at heaven. There must be some mistake!

'Why pick on me? What did I ever do to deserve this?' he cried.

It wasn't what was supposed to happen!

'I was one of the good men!' he yelled.

When nobody answered, the fury drained out of him and he started to laugh. It was a joke, a giant, cosmic joke, the best joke of all! And it was on him! He laughed until he had no more breath for laughing and his laughter rang round the mountain, out over the lake and up into the silent sky.

The avalanche had carried away his money, his gold, the evidence of his guilt, his hopes, his future.

'What d'you say now, Sarah? Still think I've got what I deserved?'

But the voice in his ear was silent and only now did he realize that it had never been Sarah's in the first place, because she was incapable of saying any of the things he'd heard her say.

That voice in his head had been his. It belonged to a part of himself that had chased away the good man he used to be.

He got off his horse, sat on a rock, took out his tobacco, rolled himself a cigarette and waited for Sheriff Colhoun to come and get him.

THE END